THE
BEGINNING

"The mission is going to take time," said General Blackford, "And a lot of American boys are going to bleed and die. It's a damn shame. Unfortunately that's war."

Patch drained his glass and put it on the bar. "There is another way." He said it without really thinking, giving voice to a thought that had been tossing around in his mind for some time.

"Another way?" asked Blackford.

Patch wanted to back off. It was something you kicked around over a bottle in the B.O.Q. Not the sort of thing a career officer puts to a general. At a general's cocktail party. Not this general.

"Well?" Blackford insisted.

Patch took the drink the PFC handed him. "What if we killed Adolf Hitler?"

THE
PATCH UNIT

Norman G. Bailey

Ace/Stoneshire Books London

First Published in the U.S.A by Tower Publications Inc.

© 1981 by Norman G. Bailey

First Ace/Stoneshire Paperback 1983

Printed in the U.K

1

Charles Patch turned the collar of his trenchcoat up. He'd passed through Fort Bliss, Texas, some years earlier, in the summer. It was hotter than hell. One hundred and twenty degrees in the shade. And, as the old saying went, no shade. And now, in February, it was colder than hell. The constant wind whipped the fine sand, and mixed with the biting grit there were snowflakes.

El Paso Del Norte. The Pass of the North. How many soldiers had come and gone over the years, cursing the weather and their fate? But then it was a very old fort.

He glanced at his watch. The invitation had said four and it was nearly four-thirty. From the cars it was the corner house. It'd been a fair walk. But they'd said to do a lot of walking.

The limp was almost completely gone. The ache was still there, though. And probably always would be to some degree, they'd said, especially in cold weather. Even when a bullet misses the bone and does its least, it's still like punching a hole in meat, and things are seldom quite the same. And there'd been two 9-mm rounds that'd gone through his left thigh less than the width of his hand apart.

The weather was miserable that Sunday, too.

After Sicily he'd returned to North Africa where he was assigned to the U.S. Sixth Corps and given command of an infantry company. The Sixth made up the southern force of the Fifth Army, under General Mark Clark, being marshalled for Operation Avalanche, the invasion of the Italian mainland near Salerno.

They sailed from Oran, Algeria, and early on September 9, 1943, stormed the beaches, assaulting with the Thirty-sixth Division followed by the Forty-fifth.

The Germans, with eight divisions in the area and a heavy proportion of armor, were expecting them and hit them with a series of counterattacks that nearly threw them back into the sea. Patch lost twenty-three men, dead, wounded or missing, in the first three hours alone.

By nightfall, though, the beachheads were four miles deep, and a dangerous gap at the Sele River was closed the following day.

After some particularly vicious fighting on the 13th and 14th — some hand-picked German troops had penetrated to within a mile of the beach—they finally began to advance. Naples fell on October 1.

As they advanced German resistance gradually stiffened. Progress became slow and painful. New divisions arrived, but at the same time the Germans hastily reinforced their own defenses.

In mid-October they crossed the Volturno River after hard fighting; and the Germans withdrew to their winter line, the Gustav line, destroying every bridge and culvert en route. Now the heavy rains and snows began, and the conflict became a slogging stalemate. It was here, near the Liri River, in the push for Cassino and the corridor to Rome that Patch took the two rounds in the leg, and but for the smile of fortune would have taken more and gone home to Arlington instead of a Texas hospital.

6

There was a heavy ground fog that morning, which began peacefully enough with only the occasional crack of small-arms fire off in the distance. A gutty young chaplain, no more than twenty-two or twenty-three, was making his way through the muddy trenches and crude forward bunkers, pausing with those who wanted to talk, and smiling or nodding to those who didn't. Patch didn't, but he could have hugged the young man for the effect he was having on the troops, many of whom were nearly old enough to be the chaplain's father. They'd all been in the line far, far too long.

Suddenly there was a roaring, whispering wind, and all hell broke loose. Patch had been shoveling mud from the entrance of the bunker he shared with his executive officer, a second lieutenant by the name of Martin.

The sleeping Martin came awake wide-eyed. "Eighty-eights," he screamed, as though an explanation were needed.

Patch drove into the bunker, and he and Martin huddled as far back as they could get. The earth trembled violently. The scrap timbers overhead moved and dirt sifted down on top of them. The barrage continued, and with it the fear of being buried alive. Minutes passed. Finally, for some unexplainable, instinctive reason Patch went back outside. Martin followed.

Some five or six feet away, the young chaplain was sitting, muddy water almost covering his legs. There was a small hole on one side of his forehead. His eyes were dull and lifeless, but otherwise there was an expression on his face that could only be described as a silly grin.

Between the shell bursts they could hear it. The dreaded clanking sound. They looked at each other and scrambled into the next bunker.

"You call in the shelling?" Martin asked Corporal

Henry.

"Yessir." The skinny radioman wiped dirt from his face.

"Get battalion," said Patch. "Fast."

A mud-soaked sergeant stuck his head in the bunker. "Captain, there's tanks . . ."

"I know," said Patch.

"Battalion, sir." Henry handed over the set. "Colonel Best."

"Patch here. We've got tanks forming on us. We're going to need some help damn quick. Over."

The voice on the other end crackled. "Reserve's taken several direct hits, Patch. They're out of it. What's your manpower, heavy weapons? Over."

"Just over two-thirds strength before this started. I don't know now. Four bazookas. Two heavy machine guns. One mortar. Maybe. Over."

An eighty-eight round landed close. The bunker shook, and dirt poured in.

"Say again. Over." Patch put a hand over his other ear.

Again the crackling. "We can't pull anyone else out of the line yet until we know how wide the front is. But we've got a 37-mm antitank outfit moving up from division reserve. I'll run 'em straight to you. Can you hold? Over."

"We'll try," said Patch. "Tell them to hurry. We can't hold long. Over."

"That's a roger. Over."

"Dog Company over and out." He gave the set back to Corporal Henry, took a deep breath and let it out. "Well, gentlemen." He relayed the situation.

"Shit," said the muddy sergeant. "Those fuckin' Panzers get to rolling and they'll have the general and

8

division for lunch." He was a very old hand of nineteen who'd served with Patch in North Africa.

Martin looked at the sergeant, but didn't say anything.

Patch smiled. "You volunteering again, Holt?"

"Don't see why not, sir." There was a hint of amusement in his eyes. "It sure as hell ain't safe around here."

Patch nodded. "Get two bazookas and half a dozen rockets each. Sidearms. Bayonets. Nothing else."

"Gotcha," said Holt, and he was off.

"I'll go," said Martin.

"You handle things here," said Patch.

They moved outside again, and PFC Bronski from the third platoon came splashing up to them, pointing out into the fog. "I think I heard . . ." he started.

"We know," said Martin.

"Have all platoon leaders report to the lieutenant," said Patch.

"And one man from every squad out and looking," added Martin. "Everybody else at the ready. Get it done, soldier."

PFC Bronski moved off at a crouching, sloshing run.

"I'll put Smith, and probably Bronski on the other two bazookas," said Martin. "Crank the mortar close and center until we can see what we're shooting at. And hold the MGs."

Patch nodded his approval. Martin was ROTC and had gone into Salerno green, but that was a lifetime ago. "If we don't stop them, and you don't stop them, then get the men down in the narrowest part of the trenches and just let them roll over you."

Martin swallowed. "Right."

"And then come up shooting quick. Do everything but burn the bores out of those fifties."

"But if you're not back, the field of fire . ."

9

"If we're not back by then, we're either not coming back or we've found a hole."

Once more into the breach, thought Patch, as he and Holt moved out into the swirling fog of no-man's land. And the old gut feeling of fear and exhilaration.

A short round landed off to the right and they both went down. Debris rained across them, and then they were off and moving again.

The clanking stopped. The tanks had advanced as far as they could without exposing themselves to their own artillery fire. In moments the barrage would lift. The attack would begin.

Patch and Holt tried to hurry. The going was hard and quickly became worse. The terrain sloped gently downhill from where they were dug in and soon they were in ankle-deep mud that sucked at their boots with each step.

"There," said Patch, hauling up short.

"Would you look at that," said Holt.

Some seventy or so yards away, and to the right, there were four Panzer III tanks lined up one just behind the other astride a low earthen dam that angled across the worst of the muddy lowland like a narrow country road. The fog gave them a ghostly appearance. The commander of each was standing in the turret. The engines were rumbling.

Three hundred twenty-horsepower Maybach gasoline engines. Capable of thrusting the nine foot tall, twenty-ton tank to twenty-five miles per hour. And with a crew of five, two and a half inches of frontal armor plate, a Krupp fifty-millimeter cannon, and two machine guns, it was indeed a wicked piece of machinery. As those who'd crossed swords with Rommel's Afrika Corps would attest.

"The first, then the last," said Patch. "Then run like hell."

"Got you."

The German in the lead tank turret turned and yelled to the other three tank commanders.

"What's that about?" asked Holt.

"Something about the shelling supposed to have quit before now. He's cursing the dummkopf flak crews."

There was some more yelling, then a hand signal.

"Oh, oh," said Patch. "They're moving forward anyway, so they can spread out."

Tank engines roared. Manual gears shifted.

Patch and Holt fired at almost the same time. Their rockets struck low and near the front of the lead Panzer III, blowing the track completely off. The machine quickly floundered in the soft earth.

Hatches slammed shut. There was a moment's hesitation. Then the other three Panzers roared into reverse in an attempt to flee the building trap. The turret of the downed tank began slowly traversing.

Holt fired. His rocket hit the rear Panzer III low, almost ground level. Parts flew, but the tank continued moving.

Patch forced himself to take his time, then fired. The 3.5 projectile struck the upper track area, just below the turret. Buckling and rippling, the severed track fed itself into the air and off the tank. "That's it," he said. "Let's go."

"You don't have to say it twice."

There was some yelling. The commander of the lead Panzer III was again standing in the turret. He was pointing at them. A heavy machine gun sounded.

They flattened into the oozing mud. Bullets slapped near Patch's head. Holt screamed and clutched his side.

11

Patch lay motionless.

As suddenly as it'd started the eighty-eight shelling stopped. There was an eerie silence. The German started down from the tank.

Quickly Patch got the sobbing sergeant up and across his shoulder, and moved off into the fog in a sliding, stumbling attempt at a run. Holt was considerably taller and heavier than the medium-framed Patch.

A couple of rounds floated close, light stuff this time, but howled away harmlessly. Patch pulled his service .45 and, without looking, squeezed off several to his rear.

"Think we're clear?" asked Holt in a quiet, strained voice.

"Don't think so." Patch was gasping for breath.

"Halt," came the command in German.

Patch turned and squeezed the trigger, knowing even as he did so that the slide was open, the handgun was empty.

The Schmeisser machine pistol spit twice, then jammed.

Patch's left leg felt like it was hit with a baseball bat. There was a burning tightness, and he thought he would go down. But he didn't. He just stood there weaving, the bleeding Holt over his shoulder, the empty .45 in hand, looking dumbly at his leg and then at the German.

With a wary eye, the German worked to clear the Schmeisser. He was a stocky bull of a man, with the rank of Unterfeldwebel.

Only seconds passed, but it seemed longer.

The German tossed the machine pistol aside, and unbuckled the flap of the black leather holster at his waist.

Patch dropped Holt and the automatic, and lunged forward, drawing a bayonet as he went. He ran the blade into the low stomach and raked upwards with both hands.

12

"*Mein Gott!*" the German screamed. He grabbed at the blade that was tearing through his intestines. One finger was sliced completely off, and the rest of his left hand was nearly cut in two.

Patch slid in the mud and went down.

Though death was in his face the German sergeant fumbled with his holster, and pulled a Luger.

A shot sounded. Then another.

The German seemed to lift up slightly out of the mud, to take a step or so backwards, and to then just fold up.

A very pale Sergeant Holt was holding his service .45 with both hands.

The German assault began as Patch staggered into the Dog Company trenches with Holt, who had now lost consciousness.

There was some quick first aid and within fifteen minutes the two were on their way to a rear field hospital, where Holt was rushed into surgery.

It was not until some two weeks later, in Naples, while awaiting shipment to the States, that Patch learned further what had happened that day from a battalion supply corporal.

The fog began to lift shortly after the German attack got under way. Initially the disabled and trapped Panzer IIIs gave fire support, but they were quickly knocked out with the arrival of the 37-mm antitank unit on the scene. That left the German infantry fighting in the difficult muddy terrain, in the open, uphill, and without heavy weapons or armored support. For a time they made a valiant effort of it, but finally withdrew after heavy losses.

Dog Company losses were light, less than five percent. Lieutenant Martin was one of these. He was killed in the initial assault wave. Second Lieutenant Gary Martin, of

Columbus, Ohio. Married to the former Ann Eppson, also of Columbus. Father of Rebecca, eight months. Whom he'd never seen.

2

A squat Mexican woman in a black dress and white apron took his trenchcoat. Somewhere a phonograph was playing "Deep in the Heart of Texas."

Patch looked around. There was a fair crowd. Everything from ninety-day wonders and their attractive young wives trying to make the right impression, to full birds and their mainly less than attractive mates trying to do the same thing.

So what're you doing here, he asked himself. Simple, he answered. When a general invites . . . But there was another reason.

He made his way through the living room and the dining room to the enclosed sunporch, where a bar was set up.

"What'll you have, Major?" The balding PFC behind the bar had to be nearly fifty.

"Whiskey and water," said Patch. "No ice."

There was an almost blurred motion and the PFC produced the drink.

"You do that well," said Patch.

"Should. I've been doing it for twenty-five years." He wiped his hands on a towel. "I lied about my age, Major. Lied in reverse, that is. One last chance for adventure, I said. And where do I end up?"

Patch smiled.

"Looks like you do some things well, too." The PFC was looking at the ribbons on Patch's jacket.

"Wrong place, wrong time," said Patch. "Several times."

A plump blond in a tight skirt came up for a refill and lingered after she got it. She was either having trouble focusing or was attempting to give Patch a seductive look.

Patch ignored her and leaned against the wall by the bar sipping his drink. He hated these damned functions. He hated this part of the army.

Finally the blond wandered off.

The whiskey was good quality. And a comfortable warmth soon replaced the chill of the Fort Bliss winter. Patch liked good whiskey, and usually kept a bottle in his footlocker for lonely evenings and quiet Sundays. But he'd drunk very little since returning stateside, and had had even less when he was across, though he'd known more than a few who'd been drunk since the North Africa landings. And that was in November of '42.

"You have any influence, Major?" The PFC took his glass and handed him another.

Patch looked at him.

"Get me where you're going, or where you've been."

"I don't know where I'm going. I'm awaiting reassignment. And where I've been . . . well, most would give their eye teeth to trade places with you. And throw in a few Purple Hearts to boot."

"I'm serious."

"So am I." Patch took a long pull on his drink. "And for that matter, I don't have much damned influence."

The colonel that she'd been talking with turned to

follow her gaze.

Adele put her hand on his arm. "I'm sorry, Jim. Thad's exec. officer from Fort Riley. I haven't . . . we haven't seen him in a long time."

"Don't place him. What's his name?"

"Patch. Charles Patch."

"Mmm. No, I don't believe so. Probably just passing through. Understand the BOQs are full of them. Like to go over and say hello?"

"In a moment. Finish telling me about your orchids first."

He smiled at the interest. He'd been stationed at Schofield Barracks in Hawaii before his transfer to Fort Bliss, and had taken up the raising of orchids as a hobby. "Well, it's not as difficult as most people think. Like I was saying, it's a matter of the right surroundings, creating a false environment as it were."

Adele tried to listen. She was truly interested. But her mind wandered.

To the windswept Kansas prairie. To the peacetime regular army. To a lieutenant called Patch.

A rogue. Good at the business of what war is about. But a misfit. The kind that is accepted by the climbers of the regular army officer corps because he would be needed. But never really accepted either.

And neither was he handsome. No, certainly not that. Rugged. Confident. Warm. Yes. But not handsome. With his chiseled Slavic features he could easily pass for an Apache Indian, were it not for the mustache. She'd never quite decided whether she liked the mustache. But then Patch wasn't the kind to have removed it for her.

He was tall. Nearly six foot four. An imposing figure. And there was about him that something, that hard to define something, that told you at once he was the leader.

Thadeous Wellington Blackford. A professor at West Point once said to him in jest that with a name like that he would surely have to become a general. He'd done just that. Brigadier General. And if the damned war would just hold out. And if he could just get to it, there would be another star.

"Logistics," he was saying. "It's like anything else. Define the problem. Define the objective. Then cut through the wasted effort. Slice out the dead wood. Use what you've got. Get what you can. And no matter what, get it done."

That was the reason for his success. He had that ability to grasp the overall situation, and to take the best possible advantage of it.

He glanced across at his wife, and then at the bar, and for a moment wondered how Patch had come to be there. His first thoughts went to Adele. But his adjutant handled the invitations. And he routinely invited the BOQ transients. A bit of good will. And undoubtedly the explanation.

"That was Rommel's trouble in Africa," said the first lieutenant.

"Exactly," said Major Willis. "Brilliant military strategy. Brilliant execution, for the most part. But they couldn't get the goods to him."

Blackford gave a nod of agreement. Patch hadn't changed. Still the street brawler quality about him. A good field soldier. But limited command potential.

"Can you imagine the possibilities," continued the major, "if Rommel'd had the general here handling his fuel and munitions?" It was not spoken as flattery, but with the genuine respect he had for his boss.

Adele had parted company with the colonel, and was

making her way over to the bar. Blackford's jaw muscle worked.

"Hello, Patch."

He'd been leaning against the bar, his back to the party, making small talk with the PFC, whose name was Mullins. He turned. And smiled. To him she was still the most beautiful woman in the world. "Hello, Adele."

For a long moment they just looked at each other. Memories.

"It's been a long time," she said finally.

He nodded. "You look good. Real good."

There was a hint of a blush. "Where . . . " She was looking at the ribbons.

"Salerno. And points north and south."

Again a pause.

"Will you be at Bliss long?"

"I'm waiting orders. Somewhere warm, I hope."

The PFC handed Patch another whiskey and water. "Something, Mrs. Blackford?"

She shook her head. "Thanks, no." Then she abruptly changed her mind. "I'll have what he's having."

Patch gave her his glass, and the PFC fixed another.

She sipped, made a face, and then laughted softly. A long forgotten moment remembered.

Neither spoke, but much was said.

They touched glasses.

Moments later they were joined by General Blackford, Major Willis, and the first lieutenant. There were introductions and handshakes.

"Well, Charles." Blackford put a hand affectionately on his wife's shoulder. "It's been a day or two since we ran the best rifle company at Fort Riley."

"That it has, sir," said Patch.

"Still Thad."

Patch had about reached that point of drinking whiskey where he knew he should stop and take a walk in the fresh air. Which is exactly what he would have done under any other circumstances.

"Been giving them hell, I see, sir," said the lieutenant, eying Patch's ribbons.

"The hell's been going both ways," said Patch.

"How good are they?" asked Major Willis. "Really."

"Finest fighting soldier on earth," said Patch.

"They're good," said Blackford. "No doubt. But they're not invincible. We laid that myth to rest along with the Afrika Corps. We're going to whip them, and we're going to do a thorough job of it."

"Amen," said Willis.

"Yes, we're going to whip them," said Patch. "After a time. And after a hell of a lot of blood's been spilled in the mud."

Blackford considered. "Yes. It's going to take time. And a lot of American boys are going to bleed and die. It's a damn shame. Unfortunately that's war."

Patch drained his glass and put it on the bar. "There is another way." He said it without really thinking, giving voice to a thought that had been tossing around in his mind for some time.

"Another way?" asked Blackford.

Patch wanted to back off. It was something you kicked around over a bottle in the B.O.Q. Not the sort of thing a career officer puts to a general. At a general's cocktail party. Not this general.

"Well?"

Adele was looking at him, too.

Patch took the drink the PFC handed him. "What if Adolf Hitler were to die?"

For a moment or so no one answered.

"Germany would collapse," said the lieutenant. "That the idea?"

"The Nazi-political system,." said Willis. "It's not really set up for a succession of power."

"Followed by a military takeover," said Patch. "And a suit for an honorable peace."

"It's possible," said Blackford. "I assume you're proposing assassination, and not just hoping for the Chancellor's early demise from ill health, bad luck, or otherwise."

"One good man with a rifle."

"Obviously it's not that simple," said Blackford.

"No sir. Not simple. But I think it could be done. With some help from the intelligence services."

"Sounds good to me, too," said the lieutenant, forgetting himself.

"Then why hasn't it been done?" asked Blackford. "Surely you don't suppose you're the only person in the entire U.S. military to have thoughts along those lines. I can see dozens of problems without even getting into it." He glanced at Willis.

"It would probably be a one-way trip, to start with," said the major. "That tends to discourage volunteers."

"You're a good man with a rifle, aren't you," said Blackford. There was a hint of malice in his voice.

"Good enough," said Patch, knowing full well he was rising to the bait.

Blackford smiled, and the mood softened. "It's an interesting theory."

The conversation took a different tack, and soon Patch was alone again at the bar. He finished his drink and left.

A long cold walk to a lonely barracks. Where he should have stayed in the first place. His thoughts were of Adele. And her truly lovely body.

21

And from that seemingly harmless exchange came a bold and gallant venture. Known in high privy circles as the biggest fuck-up in the history of warfare.

3

Hannah Müller balanced indelicately on the one-legged stool, her dress hiked high, exposing soft white thighs. Her head was bent low, and her hands worked the familiar teats with a steady rhythm sending streams of warm milk clanging into the pail.

Out of the corner of her eye she caught the switching of the tail. It came around and caught her soundly on the back of the head. She turned her head slightly, watched and waited. Again the switching. With a quick movement she caught the tail in her mouth and bit down hard.

The cow bawled loudly, moved her hind legs restlessly, and then stood quite still.

"Stupid cow," she muttered. It was always the same.

She heard the sound as she was finishing up the milking.

She gathered up the pail of milk and the basket of eggs and hurried across the barn into the adjoining kitchen. She put the fruits of her labor on the heavy oak table and took down the long-barreled Luger from its peg on the overhead beam. She switched off the safety and moved to the window.

Outside, the sun was bright on the snow. Through the huge pines, in the direction of Berchtesgaden, she caught sight of the side-car motorcycle slowly climbing, winding, on the narrow road.

Several minutes passed.

The motorcycle turned in and came to a halt near the kitchen door. The rider wore the uniform of a Sturmmann of the SS. He dismounted, removed his goggles and steel helmet, and placed them on the saddle of the motorcycle. A Schmeisser machine pistol was mounted just forward.

"Yes," said Hannah, at his knock.

He came into the kitchen. "Good morning, Hannah," he said, smiling. He was tall, blond, and very blue-eyed.

"Good morning, Willi." She pointed to the box by the door. "Fresh milk, eggs, butter and cream. For our Fuhrer, his guests, and our gallant SS."

He reproached her teasingly. "Fraülein Müller, did I hear disrespect in your voice?"

She teased him back. "But of course not." Then, more serious. "Tell me, Willi, does the Führer really eat my things?"

He shrugged. "I don't think so. His food is prepared in Berchtesgaden, then taken up to the Berghof and warmed. What I get from you goes to the SS barracks." He dug in his pocket and handed her an envelope.

She looked inside, counted, and put it in her apron.

He caught sight of the Luger on the sideboard, where she'd laid it. He picked it up. "From the Great War. An artillery model."

"My father's. He was given the Iron Cross, First Class, for his bravery on the Western Front in 1918."

"He's . . . ?"

"Dead? Yes."

Willi took off the safety, and opened the toggle far enough to see that there was a round in the chamber.

"My father always said an empty gun is next to

worthless."

Willi nodded. He put the safety on and returned the piece to the sideboard. "I've missed you, Hannah."

She smiled. "It has only been two days."

"Two days can be a long time." He came to her, took her hand, and gently coaxed her toward her bedroom.

Yes, she was thinking, two days can be a very long time.

On the outskirts of Berchtesgaden Willi turned sharply to the left, and at the foot of the Obersalzberg started up the steep, frequently icy road to the Berghof. A half-track, or even a four-wheel vehicle handled the road better, but the motor pool usually insisted on more errands, and a second man.

He passed neat snowbound farm houses, and an old church, and then passed into an area guarded by a high barbed-wire fence which could be entered only after identity checks at two gates. To Willi it was reminiscent of an open-air enclosure for wild animals.

As always, despite almost any kind of weather, there were curiosity seekers, trying to catch a glimpse of some of the prominent inhabitants of the mountain.

And, as always, Willi felt a touch of sadness on his return to the mountain. Such a scarring of the magnificent landscape. Not the Führer, of course. He, too, loved the natural beauty. The way it had been in the 1920's and early '30s.

It was Reichsleiter Martin Bormann. The man of the shadows. Inevitably present. He'd forcibly bought up centuries-old farms and had the buildings torn down. The same with numerous chapels. He'd confiscated state forests until the private area reached from the top of the mountain to the valley, and embraced an area of over two and a half square miles. The inner fence was almost two miles in length, and that around the outer perimeter some nine miles.

With total insensitivity to the natural surroundings he'd laid out a network of roads, turning forest paths into pavement. He'd built barracks, a manor house, a guest hotel, a complex for the employees, and dormitory barracks for the construction workers.

Even the tumbledown castle of Klessheim, some distance from the Berghoff, had been rebuilt into a luxurious guest house.

Willi dropped the box of foodstuff at the mess, and the motorcycle at the motor pool.

Scharenführer Meyer looked up from the file on his desk as Willi signed in. "This new directive," he said, tapping a finger. "It concerns you." He was a thickset man, a bit older than many in the SS. There was a perpetual gruffness about him that all but hid a rather amiable disposition. And this made it exceedingly difficult to tell just when he was serious, and when he was not.

Willi waited.

"I'll paraphrase, if I may. It says that henceforth, instead of the Third Reich paying you each month for your services, you will, instead, pay the Third Reich." He paused to let that soak in.

Willi frowned, but didn't reply.

"You ask the reason for this. It is because your duty station affords you a permanent holiday in Bavaria, and probably better bed and board than you had at home. And a pretty Fräulein, too, perhaps?" He closed the file.

Willi could see that it was the guard duty roster.

Meyer laughed. "I am only joking, of course. But there

26

is much in what I say, is there not?"

Willi nodded. "Have you thought about what I asked?"

"What you asked?"

"About being assigned to the Führer's personal staff."

Meyer shook his head. "Willi, Willi. You don't want that. Certainly, it's an honor and an inspiration to work so closely to him. But it's also a terrible strain. Do you know what your duties would be?"

"Some."

"Much of the time you would wear a brilliant white uniform. You would wait table. Taste his food. Anticipate his wants. And those of his guests. And always you would be an alert bodyguard."

"That doesn't sound so bad."

"No, that's not the bad part."

"Then what?"

"The pressure. To make no mistakes. Oh, the Führer is usually forgiving enough." He lowered his voice a bit. "But not the others. And you wouldn't be returned to your regular duties. It would be the Russian Front. Or worse, depending on the seriousness of your mistake. You see?"

"But there would be a grade increase, would there not?"

"Yes, Willi." Meyer sighed. "There would be an increase in rank."

And with more pay, marriage could be considered.

Meyer jumped to his feet.

Willi brought himself to attention.

"What are you doing here, Sturmmann?" Hauptsturmführer Spaatz tossed his greatcoat over the coatrack. He was a short man with flaxen hair and icy gray eyes. The decorations spoke of Russia and of wounds.

"He's just reporting in, sir," said Meyer.

"And he can probably speak for himself, too, can't he?"

"Yes, sir."

"Well?"

"Reporting in, sir. And also I was inquiring about being put on the Führer's personal staff."

The officer stepped up quite close to Willi. The Death's Head insignia gleamed. "What is your oath?"

"My honor is loyalty!"

"Are you a homosexual, Sturmmann Roehrs? The Führer abhors such."

"Nein!"

"No, I think not. I think you've been getting more than butter from Fräulein Hannah Muller." He considered for a moment, his cold eyes probing Willi. "Very well, Roehrs. There is an opening."

"Thank you, sir." Willi threw his arm high in salute, careful not to hit the officer. *"Heil Hitler."*

Hauptsturmführer Spaatz returned the salute, picked up a sheaf of papers from the incoming box on Meyer's desk and went on into his office.

With a brief smile at Meyer, Willi took his leave. It would be two days before he could tell Hannah. He could hardly wait.

Meyer picked up his pipe from the ash tray, struck a match and held it to the bowl. Müller. He'd known a Müller. In Munich. In 1933 or '34. He puffed contentedly. But then Müller was a common name.

4

At the P.O.W. administration building at Fort Bliss, Constance Adams was just finishing up another tedious initial interview. The man across the desk from her seemed kindly enough to be her grandfather. And he probably was someone's grandfather.

"That's all for today, Herr Generalmajor," she said in flawless German. "Please ask the next gentleman to come in."

The elderly general stood, did a smart to-the-right, and left the room.

The man that entered had a scar that traversed his face from his left temple to just below his right ear, running dangerously across his right eye. It had the effect both of marring the attractiveness of a rather good-looking man, and of adding to it in a romantic sort of way. He clicked his heels and bowed slightly from the waist with a touch of old-world charm.

"Please sit down," said Constance. She looked at the file in front of her. "You're Standartenführer . . ."

"Colonel Max Wolff," he said. There was a definite hint of the British Isles in his voice. "We may speak English if you like."

"You speak it rather well."

"I was two years in England. I studied medicine there.

Part of an exchange program of the time."

"You're a doctor?"

"Regrettably, I didn't finish. I hope to someday."

"I thought perhaps . . . " She was looking at the scar.

He put a finger to it. " . . . that I was part of the old Prussian dueling class? No." He laughed softly. "This is the real thing. A Russian bayonet near Stalingrad. As the Englander is fond of saying, I nearly bought it."

"Then you fought in Russia?"

He smiled at the obvious lack of subtlety to her question. "What is the purpose of the questioning, Miss . . . "

"Mrs. Constance Adams."

"Your husband is most fortunate," said Wolff. "You're a beautiful woman."

She felt the flush cross her face. She was off guard, and flustered. And she didn't like it. "Obviously we're building files on the higher ranking officers . . . "

" . . . and attempting to gain information about your enemy."

"Your cooperation, or lack of it, will be noted, and will undoubtedly be a factor after . . . "

"I will answer." Again the smile. "Selectively."

"You served with the SS in Russia?"

"Waffen SS. There is a difference."

"The elite military."

"Strictly military. Not the royal bodyguard. Not the Gestapo. Not the prison camp . . . guards."

She waited for him to continue.

"A parachute/assault unit," he said. "The first into the line. And the last out."

"What can you tell me about these other sections of the Schutzstaffel?"

He didn't answer.

"Where else have you served, Colonel Wolff?"

He took out a cigarette and a wooden match. "May I smoke?"

"Of course." She pushed an ashtray to his side of the desk.

He lighted the cigarette, and took several deep puffs, obviously enjoying it. "A Lucky Strike." He shook his head. "The Russian cigarettes were terrible. You were asking?"

"Where else you'd served."

"Mainly Russia. The Lowlands early in the war. And finally Italy."

"Where you were captured."

"Yes."

"What was your unit in Italy?"

He didn't answer.

She made a notation of his uniform markings. "Its strength?"

Again, no answer.

"Your immediate superior?"

"Constance. May I call you Constance?"

"Of course."

"I am not going to answer such questions. Undoubtedly it would have little effect now. And I, and others, may have mixed feelings about this war that my country is involved in. But I love my country. And I am loyal."

"But don't you think it would help your country . . . "

"The only thing that would help my country would be for that raving madman in the Chancellory . . . " He inhaled deeply at the stub of the cigarette and snubbed it out.

There were frequent undertones of disapproval of Adolf Hitler, but they were usually mild in expression, and usually by Wehrmacht officers, not SS officers. "Please go on, Max."

31

The use of the familiar was not lost on him. "He is leading Germany into a deep, dark abyss from which it will never return. It's that simple, Mrs. Adams."

"Then isn't it logical that anything you can do that would help to bring about an early defeat . . ."

"Possibly," he said. "Before we're overrun from the east. But I'm still not going to tell you any secrets, precious few that I might know. Illogical or not."

Constance looked at her watch. They'd run overtime. "Perhaps we can continue this discussion again another time."

"Perhaps," he said, taking the cue and rising.

On impulse she took a pack of cigarettes from her purse and gave them to him.

"Thank you, Constance." Again, the slight bow from the waist. And he left the room.

She sat back in her chair and swiveled. He'd said nothing he hadn't intended to say. And she'd learned nothing of any real value. And there was little hope for future interviews.

It was going to be another long day. Damn it to hell.

He was bald and a bit overweight. His collar was unbuttoned and his tie was loosened. His desk was piled high with files. But he had the appearance of one who is used to such paper pressure.

He was. He'd been a lawyer in civilian life.

Milly came in carrying another armload of files.

He pointed.

She balanced them there.

He raised his eyes and watched the sway of her hips as she left his office. He'd decided that his one remaining ambition in life was to take her to bed. To bed, hell. The floor, the desk, anywhere. And if he couldn't get in her

32

pants he was going to get her transferred. She was driving him crazy.

She stuck her head back in. "Ready on that call to Texas."

He picked up the phone. "General T.W. Blackford?"

"This is General Blackford."

"Lieutenant Colonel George Dalbert. Washington. Office of Strategic Services."

"Yes?"

"I have a report here that you forwarded recently. It made its way around town and ended up on my desk. Concerns a rather ambitious undertaking across the big drink. Do you . . . "

"Yes. We're on the telephone, Colonel."

"I'm aware of that, General. It's my nickel. But since you wrote the report you know what it's about. And since I have it in front of me I know what it's about. And I thought perhaps we could just discuss it in general terms. It's not all that specific anyway."

"It's a proposal which I feel warrants consideration."

"Certainly it warrants consideration. But it's hardly a new concept. This office has been toying with it since 1940."

"But you haven't got it done, have you?"

"No, sir. But unless there's something that makes this different . . . "

"The man," said Blackford.

"The man?"

"A very able infantry officer whom I know personally."

"That this Patch you refer to?"

"Major Patch. Combat experienced. Highly decorated."

"Still, with all due respect to Major Patch . . . "

"He believes very strongly that it can be done, Colonel."

"Hell's bells, General, there've been more than one or two who believed strongly that they could fly — without benefit of a plane or what have you."

"You're not a soldier by trade, are you, Dalbert?" Blackford asked quietly.

"No, but I certainly don't see what that has to . . . "

"Battles, campaigns, and sometimes even wars are won by those who have the balls to try and do what they believe they can do."

"You apparently feel strongly about this, too."

"The stakes are high. As the major pointed out, a hell of a lot of good men are going to die, otherwise. Seems like it just might be worth a try."

There was a moment's silence.

"Perhaps so," said Dalbert. "Perhaps so. Tell you what. I've got a man on his way to your part of the country now. Going to talk to some of those high-level P.O.W.s you have out there. I'll have him meet with you and this Major Patch and then give me a feasibility report. If it's top quality I'll kick it upstairs with recommendations. Otherwise . . . "

"We're in agreement, Colonel."

"And I'll keep you advised."

"I'd appreciate that."

Dalbert felt a little like he'd just lost a case when he put the phone down.

Milly came in with more files.

"Looks like late work tonight," he said.

"Oh, dear." She made a bit of a face.

"Problem?"

"Date."

"Oh. Well, you go ahead."

She gave him a smile and hurried out, her bottom undulating.

He watched her go. Finally he turned to another file. Later he would take a cold shower and have a tall drink.

5

A periscope parted the murky water. It traversed to seaward, and then slowly began to study the French coastline.

Finally the submarine surfaced. Hatches opened silently. The cannon was quickly manned, and the conning tower watch taken. Out of its element now, the boat rode roughly, pitching abruptly sideways. Wet metal glinted in the hazy moonlight. Minutes passed.

Four men appeared on deck. A raft was readied, eased into the water, and held alongside. They watched the coastline.

One was the youthful commander of the submarine.

The other three wore dark clothing, and their faces were smudged with burnt cork. Each carried a Browning fourteen shot 9mm semiautomatic pistol in a shoulder holster. There were extra clips, Fairbairn-Sykes knives, and other various tools of their trade.

"This is the worst of it, isn't it, mate," said the leader of the commandos. "Sitting-duck time." His name was Percival Hastings and he was a sergeant-major in the British army. He was a professional soldier, though he'd spent much of his youth as a merchant seaman. A large rawboned man with a brush mustache, he'd once been requested to pose for a recruiting poster. He'd declined.

36

The sub commander smiled. "Always a bit dicey on top. And I don't envy you chaps either."

"It's not so bad, once we get moving," said the commando holding the bow line of the raft. He was Philip Joubert, and, in a word, he was short and fat. An unlikely looking specimen, but he'd been on a number of such forays, most of them with Hastings. He was a French national, a civilian, a butcher by trade. Somewhere, at one time in northeast France in a village near Reims, there was a wife and three sons in their middle teens. Earlier on, an occasional word had drifted out. But for a long time now, nothing. "It's the waiting," he said.

The third commando, holding the stern line, was quiet. The others were afraid, but Private Lammers's fear showed. Too much. All commandos are volunteers, but Lammers should not have been accepted. He was seeking the courage he admired in others. A fine thing. But he really hadn't the stomach for it. And such men are dangerous. For they are always too close to that brink of uncontrollable fear. And thus they are never really reliable. But to refuse to accept such a "mate," and there is always that choice, is to totally destroy the man.

"Is this one hush-hush," asked the sub commander, "or can I inquire. Just curious, you know." An able seaman brought him a second, larger pair of binoculars.

"Resistance leader went sour," said Hastings. "Have to teach the bloody beggar a lesson."

The Frenchman drew a finger across his throat.

"You're just going to kill him?" asked the seaman.

Hastings smiled thinly. "He turned in his group, son. Yesterday morning thirteen men and four women were lined up against a wall."

"Oh." The seaman seemed to pale.

"The only one left is running," said Joubert. "Man-

37

aged to get word to us."

"That the one meeting you?" asked the sub commander.

Hastings nodded.

"Any chance it's a trap?"

"Oui, monsieur. Always."

Hastings put a hand on Lammers's shoulder. "Once they get the last one, the leader's free to tell some tales and infiltrate another group."

"Why you chaps? Why not some other local people?"

"Only the leaders have much outside contact. Members usually just know a code name. And when something like this starts. . ." Joubert shrugged. "No one knows who to trust."

"Signal, sir," came the call from the conning tower. "Starb'd beam landward."

There were three long flashes, followed by three short.

"That's us," said Hastings. "We're off."

The three commandos climbed down into the raft.

"I'll stay at periscope until first light," said the sub commander. "But if you're not back by then . . . " He made a futile gesture with his hands.

Hastings nodded.

"God be with you."

The commandos pushed off. As soon as they were clear the submarine slipped back beneath the surface. And though, for a time at least, they could see the periscope, there was a very ominous feeling of being alone.

"It's always tough," said Hastings softly, "even when you've done it a dozen times."

Lammers tried to smile his appreciation, but that brought on a nervous tic to one eye and he put his back into rowing.

The sea was not what would be considered heavy, but it would have been hard to convince the men in the raft of that.

They stopped speaking when they were still some distance out, and made every effort to be silent with the oars.

Joubert pointed to a shadowy outcropping of rock. Hastings nodded. They made for it.

As they drew close Joubert went over the side. He lost his footing, went under, and bobbed up again. Hastings and Lammers went into the water.

They beached the raft on a slide of black shale. It was all but invisible, at least until morning.

Joubert located a stump of piling, and started down the beach, almost in the surf, taking carefully measured steps.

Lammers hadn't known about this, but quickly understood the significance. He was wide-eyed.

Hastings tried to give him a look of confidence, but it was hard. He was scared silly himself.

Joubert turned abruptly inland, walking a very straight line. Lammers followed. Hastings brought up the rear, duck-walking and smoothing out their footsteps behind him with his hand.

A barely audible sigh from Joubert told them that they were through the minefield. Or at least that they were supposed to be.

Then, as one, they flattened onto the seaward side of a sand dune. Close by, very close, a man with a large dog on a tether was standing, watching them. The shape of the helmet said it all.

Or was he watching them? He'd made no move to unsling his rifle. And the dog certainly hadn't detected them yet.

Lammer's hand eased to the butt of his Browning. Joubert stopped him.

They waited.

Finally the man and the dog moved on.

Another minute or so passed. The soaked clothing and the chill of the winter night had its effect. There were spasms of trembling. The circumstances undoubtedly contributed.

Then, suddenly, just across the road that ran along the beach, someone stood and began waving at them.

They looked at each other.

"I'll go," said Hastings. He thumbed the safety off the already cocked Browning, and went forward, slowly, ready to drop at the slightest hint of trouble. But then he knew, too, that if it were a trap there probably wouldn't be any warning. Well, they'd better make it both quick and good or he'd damn well take this bloody beggar with him.

"The moon is blue," said the slight figure as he approached.

Hastings smiled. "Yes, it most certainly is." The contact was a girl. A pretty young thing, no more than fifteen or sixteen. "Winston sends his best."

Hannah Müller, a wool blanket around her, came back into the bedroom with a steaming mug of coffee in her hand. Not ersatz. The real thing. She blew on it. The aroma was absolutely beautiful. She took a sip.

From the bed Willi watched her. The covers were up around his chin. It'd snowed during the night, and it was still overcast. And the normally cold bedroom was even colder.

She handed him the mug.

He took it and propped himself up on one elbow.

40

"Why didn't you say something before you did it?" she asked.

"I thought you would be pleased."

"Pleased? We'll see each other even less."

"But the promotion is automatic. There'll be more money, and we can be married."

She looked at him.

"I want to be your husband, Hannah."

"In these times . . . " she started.

"The war can't last forever. It's going badly. Very badly. From what I hear at . . . "

"One doesn't have to be at the Berghof to know that."

He put the mug on the nightstand and reached for her.

She stepped back just a bit. "And like your sergeant says, if you cross someone up there you'll be sent to the front."

"I won't."

"Can you be so sure? Some of the things I've heard . . ."

"I'm sure." He lay back. "After the war we'll live here." He had a faraway look. "I'll be a woodcutter. And there'll be children."

Her mood softened, despite herself.

He smiled. "Can't you see it? Little Hannah. Little Willi."

She almost laughed. But the thought pleased her too.

He got out of bed and came to her. "I love you, Hannah."

"Oh, Willi. I love you, too."

The blanket dropped to the floor.

6

At a signal, Joubert and Lammers came forward.

"I'm Colette," she said. "The traitor is in the village. A short way." At that she took off, like a cross-country runner.

The commandos followed. Across fields and dikes. Along canals and hedgerows. At least the running warmed them, and dried their clothing somewhat.

When she stopped, they were on the outskirts of a small village that Hastings remembered from the maps as Rouge something or something Rouge. A farming and fishing village, just like hundreds of others that dotted the French coastline.

"If we're seen," she said, "it will be bad. The curfew."

Somewhere, a dog was barking.

They entered the village, and then a narrow alley. Near the far end they stopped in the shadows between two ancient three-story buildings.

Colette pointed to the one. "La Taverne Du Dauphin. He's in a room on the second floor. But some soldiers of the coast patrol are billeted there too."

"How many at any one time?" asked Hastings.

"Maybe eight or ten."

"Mmm," said Joubert.

They looked at him.

He smiled. "Smell the wine."

"Good God," said Hastings. "Stairs," he asked the girl.

"From the front. In the cafe. But there will be soldiers there too. Most of the night."

"Then there's no way . . . " started Lammers.

Joubert was looking up. Directly above, a dormer window came out of the roof. "The third floor?" he asked.

"Unoccupied," said Colette. "For many years. It leaks too badly."

"And there?" He looked to the other building. There was a window just opposite the dormer window.

"Apartments. I think that's a hallway."

"We'll need a good sturdy board," said Hastings. He and Joubert were thinking as one. It frequently happened. "Like the scaffolding that painters and carpenters use."

Colette thought for a moment, and then nodded.

They located the plank, and made their way to the top floor of the apartment house, though not without a bit of noise, what with the size of their burden and the narrow, winding, creaking stairs. But the times were such that tenants were not inclined to investigate footsteps in the halls.

The hall window did indeed look straight across to the dormer window of La Taverne Du Dauphin. They put the board across.

"Two go and two stay?" asked Joubert.

"No," said Hastings, "we'll stay together." If things got sticky, Lammers was questionable. And Colette would be needed as a guide. He stepped out onto the board, and tried not to look down. The feeling of being three stories above an alley was there nevertheless. There was a slight

43

but unsettling bounce with each step, and in the middle a definite sag.

On the other side he eased the window open. A partially broken pane of glass fell out. He juggled it, and then held on to it.

Inside, he stepped quickly to one side of the window.

There was a sudden flurry of motion across the room.

He dropped to a crouch, drew the Browning and almost squeezed the trigger. But he didn't. He set the piece of glass down and took out a pencil flashlight. Holding it away from his body he flicked it on and then off again.

Rats.

He sighed and smiled, and returned the piece to its holster. Hard to believe the bloody beggars could be welcome. But they would be the natural explanation for any third-floor noises.

He motioned to the others.

Colette came across quickly, almost gracefully. Lammers was slower, but handled it well.

Hastings was thinking how light on his feet Joubert was for a man of his build when it happened.

The Frenchman was just past the halfway point. There was a crackling sound, much like the report of a light caliber rifle. And thus a brief warning. He dove for the window. For a moment his fingers clutched the sill, then slid to the roof tiles just beneath. The board crashed to the alley below.

Hastings reached out and grabbed an arm, and might have gone out the window if Lammers hadn't anchored him around the waist.

More off the roof than on, Joubert tried to reach up and firm up his lifeline, and in so doing almost pulled himself loose from Hastings' grasp altogether.

A door directly below opened. Briefly the area was lighted. Long enough to note the field gray of the uniform. The door closed. The man stepped to the middle of the alley. He seemed to be looking around. Then he undid his trousers and began to urinate.

Hastings' arms felt like they were coming out of the sockets. Silently, Colette took Lammers' place at his waist, though she couldn't weigh much more than a full field pack. Lammers leaned out and took hold of Joubert's other arm.

The man belched, and continued to urinate. Finally he tucked himself back in and buttoned his trousers. He took one more look around, apparently oblivious to the piece of broken plank he'd just urinated on. He went back inside.

They quickly hauled Joubert up into the room.

"Mother of God," he said, rubbing his arms. "I've never know a man to go so long." He made an apologetic gesture to Colette.

She giggled.

It was after two in the morning when they made their move. The best time, according to Colette.

Joubert took the lead, Fairbairn knife in hand. They came down from the dark of the third floor, slowly, hoping against the creaking step that would sound the alarm.

There was a sentry sitting in a chair on the second-floor landing. He was facing the other direction.

Joubert went ahead. The German was evidently dozing. He came up right behind him and jerked the helmet back, cutting off all but a quiet gagging sound. A foolish thing for a soldier to wear a helmet strap under the chin. Joubert drew the knife across his throat. There was a gurgling. Then silence.

They took the body part way up the third floor stairs,

and propped it on a step. Lammers remained with the corpse. From the shadows of the "high ground" he could effectively control the second-floor landing as well as the approach to it from the ground floor.

Colette led Hastings and Joubert down the second-floor hallway, to the last door on the right. She pointed, grimly.

Joubert put the girl behind him. Standing to one side Hastings tried the door. It was unlocked. He was immediately suspicious. But then things are seldom what one expects. He let the door swing open.

In a bed on the far side of the room a partially clothed man was sleeping. The woman beside him, totally nude, was awake. She looked at her companion, and at the commandos, and seemed to understand what was happening. She was terrified.

The room was lighted by a candle in a wine bottle on the nightstand, and the flickering yellow light made the scene all the more eerie.

Hastings touched the blade of his knife to his lips.

The woman's eyes said she understood, and that she would be silent.

He glanced at Colette for confirmation.

She nodded.

He started across the room. A board creaked.

The man's eyes came open.

Hastings moved quickly. He clasped a hand across the man's mouth, and slashed his throat.

The man strained upwards, and then fell back. His eyes begged. And then went vacant.

The woman cringed as far away in the bed as she could get.

Joubert came around, grabbed her by her long black hair, and began whacking it off close to the scalp.

"There's no time . . . " started Hastings.

But Joubert was quickly finished with the telltale haircut. "For a time, at least," he said, "everyone will know." He held up the knife. "I'm going to wait outside the door, *ma chérie*. Maybe one second. Maybe one hour. If you make a sound, or come out, and I'm still there, I'm going to cut you from here to here."

She shuddered as he gestured with the knife, pricking her skin.

They closed the door quietly behind them, leaving the sobbing woman on the blood-spattered bed.

What they found down the hall turned the headiness of a dangerous mission going well into the kind of fear that clutches at your throat.

From the long shadow, a man was standing just a step or two below the second-floor landing, probably puzzling over the empty sentry's chair. And, if you knew where to look, Lammers had a Browning 9 mm aimed at him. He was holding the piece in two hands, shaking slightly, and it seemed as though he were about to squeeze the trigger.

Both Hastings and Joubert began frantically shaking their heads, pointing to their knives.

With the element of surprise they could just suddenly step into the cafe below, control the situation, and make their escape. But if —

Lammers was not to be swayed. The Browning exploded. In the confines of the hall it sounded like a small cannon. Not satisfied with that, he squeezed off another one.

A body tumbled down the steps.

For a long moment afterwards there was silence.

Then the woman began to scream. A door opened nearby.

Joubert threw a quick shot.

The door slammed shut.

47

"I'll take the point," said Hastings, starting down the stairs. "You keep them off our backs."

Joubert nodded.

At that point Lammers lost complete control. He went hurtling past Hastings, knocking Colette aside. At the bottom of the steps there was a sharp left turn, and he disappeared from view.

There were three shots. Lighter than a 9 mm.

Lammers came back into view, clutching his stomach. He sat down at the bottom of the steps.

Hastings got down on his belly and let himself slide headfirst down the stairs.

In the cafe a German officer was standing, pointing his Walther PPK like an offhand target shooter. He was apparently expecting his next adversary to be as foolhardy as the last.

Hastings and the German fired at the same time.

The 7.65 mm rounds went wide. The 9 mm didn't. The German officer was slammed backwards against the bar, and went down.

There were three soldiers at a table. They were unarmed, and had their hands up.

Hastings hesitated as he went by. If he didn't kill them, they would shortly be trying to kill him. "I'm sorry," he said. And he shot the three point-blank.

Lammers came through the cafe leaning heavily on Colette. Near the door his eyes rolled back, and he collapsed.

For a moment she bent over him. But nothing.

There was a burst of submachine gun fire in the stairwell. But Joubert emerged unscathed. He glanced at Lammers, and grabbed Colette by the hand.

As they left the cafe both Hastings and Joubert threw a good half dozen rounds each back at the stairs. To help buy just a bit of time.

They ran.

Between houses. Through a wintery orchard. Past an old barn.

With the village behind them, there came a vague sense of safety. But it wasn't over.

They slowed as they neared the beach. The coast patrol would have heard the gunfire, and would be particularly alert.

"There," said Colette, when they'd crossed the coast road. It was the way through the minefield to the surf.

"You're not coming?" asked Joubert.

"No," she said.

"Sure?" asked Hastings.

She smiled. "I'm sure."

Then there was a long moment that only those who have served with another under fire would understand. Nothing was said. Nothing need be said. They might never see each other again, but they would be comrades forever.

They parted.

Hastings and Joubert were wading the raft into the surf when they heard the mournful plea.

"Wait . . . wait . . . "

It was Lammers' voice, but —

A flashlight came on, catching Colette and Lammers, almost to the surf, almost across the mined area of the beach. Then a large dog ran into the minefield toward them, its tether flopping behind.

"Nein, Schultz, nein!" The German soldier was too close.

Lammers pushed Colette down, and flung himself across her.

The dog literally exploded.

The flashlight went out.

Joubert held the raft, and Hastings hurried ashore.

Lammers was destroyed. There could be no question this time. Colette was alive. But just barely. Hastings picked her up gently, like the small child that she almost was.

Soon the raft was pulling for the open sea. Flashlights seemed to come on everywhere. Rifles cracked. But they had the safety of distance now.

The submarine had surfaced and was waiting for them when they reached it. Its commander was on the deck. "Hurry," he said. "There's a patrol boat in the area."

Hastings handed the girl up to him, and he and Joubert climbed aboard. The boat was immediately under way. The raft drifted free.

The sub commander felt Colette's wrist, and then her neck. "This one's dead," he said.

"No . . . " started Hastings.

Joubert knelt and put a hand on the slender throat. "*Oui*, my friend. She's gone."

"She's closing fast," came the call from the conning tower.

"Dive!" said the sub commander. "After you, gentlemen. Please don't dally."

Hastings glanced back as he scrambled up the conning tower ladder. The deck was awash now. Colette slipped into the sea.

Below, when the dive was complete, and the safety of the depths reached, the commandos were given blankets and a ration of rum.

"This bloody fucking war," said Hastings. His eyes were red. "Do you know who the man was? The one in the bed?"

Joubert and the sub commander looked at him.

"Colette's father. That's right. The traitor was Colette's father." He drank his rum, and turned away.

7

Captain David Weinberg, OSS, was given the message to call Washington almost as soon as he stepped off the plane at El Paso. His first thought was that something might be wrong with his wife or one of his small children.

Lieutenant Colonel Dalbert filled him in, in guarded language, as to the gist of General Blackford's report and the subsequent telephone conversation. And thus it was that Weinberg found himself waiting in General Blackford's outer office. He rather guessed that the beribboned major sitting across from him was the Charles Patch that Colonel Dalbert had referred to.

Patch, on the other hand, had no idea why he'd been summoned to General Blackford's office. He'd given no further thought to the remarks he'd made at the general's cocktail party. Maybe an assignment was in the offing. That'd be damned welcome.

He glanced at the captain on the other side of the room. A pleasant-looking young fellow. A non-professional, though. A staff type. Probably come out of the war with more rank than he would.

Major Willis stuck his head out of the inner office. "Gentlemen, the general will see you now."

Inside, they saluted. There were introductions. And they were waved into some fairly comfortable chairs.

The not-so-young PFC Mullins who'd tended bar at the general's cocktail party served coffee, and then took his leave.

Blackford lighted a cigar. Blue smoke curled toward the desk lamp and then up to the ceiling. "If Adolf Hitler could be successfully assassinated," he said. "If. Charles thinks it can be done." There was a small, framed photograph of Adele on the desk.

"I'd like to hear the plan," said Weinberg.

Patch took a deep breath. He wasn't prepared for this. He'd never really thought it all out. "It's not so much a plan," he said.

They looked at him.

"Well, it goes something like this. A man goes into an area that Hitler's known to frequent. He holes up with a local citizen. One who can be trusted, and who'll keep him advised of what's happening. When the opportunity presents itself he adapts himself to the circumstances. Bang."

There was a long silence, as though something very complicated had just been explained in simple terms.

"A good man with a rifle," said Blackford.

"One or two good men," said Patch. "And a small arsenal of weapons. Flexibility's the key."

"How would the men get out?" asked Weinberg.

"How about 'safe-houses'?" asked Patch. "The same way downed pilots make their way out."

Weinberg nodded.

"What do you estimate the survival chances at?" asked Willis.

"Probably not much worse than a heavy firefight up front."

"He's obviously heavily guarded," said Willis.

"At times unbelievably so," said Weinberg. "But there

are times when he frustrates his guards, too. The worst thing is, he seems to lead a charmed life. It's been tried before."

"There should be more than two men," said Blackford. "One might be killed or injured, or get sick. They should be able to break into teams if the situation calls for it."

Patch nodded his agreement.

Weinberg was up and pacing the room. "Berchtesgaden," he said. "That's the place. He spends more time there than anywhere else. Rural. Mountainous, Timber." He smiled at Patch. "Snowstorms."

"Sounds good," said Patch.

"You've been there?" asked Blackford.

"Several times, with my uncle, before the war." Weinberg helped himself to a cigar from Blackford's desk, lighted it, and resumed his pacing.

Blackford leaned back in his chair, a trace of amusement in his eyes.

"Sprechen Sie Deutsch, Herr Patch?" asked Weinberg.

"Ich spreche etwas . . . Probably enough . . . "

"No," said Weinberg. "At least one of the team would have to be absolutely fluent. For safety. To talk them through whatever they might run into."

"You?" asked Blackford.

"I'm not that good," said Weinberg.

"Maybe a German soldier," said Patch. "That could help in a lot of ways."

"Yes," said Weinberg.

Willis smiled. "One that doesn't like Hitler."

"There should be one or two around," said Blackford. "Probably right here at Bliss."

"Damn!" Weinberg stopped pacing, and put his hands

54

on his hips. "This has possibilities. Rough spots, to be sure. But nothing the people upstairs shouldn't be able to smooth out."

"Then time's of the essence, isn't it," said Blackford. He picked up the telephone. "Get me Washington. Office of Strategic Services." He handed the phone to Weinberg.

Hauptsturmführer Hans Spaatz stepped from the motorcycle sidecar. It was snowing somewhat heavier now. And the air was fresh, and clean, and crisp. He breathed deeply.

There were lights here and there. But then much of the Berghof operated twenty-four hours a day.

His driver, SS-Mann Kruger, dismounted, a bit weary it seemed, and threw his arm in salute. "Will that be all, sir?" He was obviously chilled to the bone.

Spaatz returned the salute. Cold. Russia was cold. This was invigorating. But Kruger was a good enough soldier. A little young, and not yet hard. But with time he would be the kind of soldier any man would be proud to serve with. "See that this machine is given the proper maintenance when you return it."

"Tonight, sir?"

Spaatz didn't answer, but merely looked at him.

"Yes, sir." Kruger climbed back aboard, kicked the motorcycle to life, and moved off in the direction of the motor pool, slipping and sliding.

Inside, Scharenführer Meyer jumped to his feet. Another soldier was already standing at attention. Spaatz removed his greatcoat and tossed it over the coatrack.

"Did you have a satisfactory tour, sir?" asked Meyer.

"Routine." Spaatz glanced at the soldier, and then to Meyer.

"I regret to report," said the Scharenführer, "that Sturmmann Beck was found asleep at his post." He looked at the wall clock. "One hour and fifteen minutes ago."

There was a long, dangerous silence.

Then Spaatz stepped close to the soldier. Very deliberately he unbuckled the gleaming black holster at his waist and drew his Luger. He thumbed the safety off and touched the muzzle to Beck's temple. "There can be no excuse for failing your Fatherland in such a manner." He said it softly. His finger tightened on the trigger.

"No, sir," said Beck. The tremor started with his lip as he spoke, and spread over his body. This was more than understandable, as a Luger is not known for its crisp trigger pull as a target pistol is.

"The Eastern Front, sir?" asked Meyer.

Another long moment passed.

There was a click as the weapon was returned to safety. Beck jumped.

"Tonight," said Spaatz. "A unit that's been in the line a very long time."

"I'll cut the orders immediately, Hauptsturmführer. He'll be on his way within the hour."

"Now get this swine out of my sight!"

"Get out!" yelled Meyer.

Sturmmann Beck ran from the room.

"You were going to shoot him, weren't you, sir."

Spaatz merely looked at him. "The road to the Castle Klessheim?"

"Yes, sir?"

"The patrol is predictable. Work out a staggering schedule. Have it on my desk as soon as possible."

"Jawohl."

Spaatz stepped into his office and closed the door with his boot.

He took a rag from a desk drawer and wiped the Luger down. It was a beautiful piece. George Luger's pistol design of 1908. Absolutely the finest weapon ever made. Not as modern as the Walthers. But more powerful than the PP or PPK. And every bit as reliable as the P-38 as long as it was kept clean. This was an older one. A Death's Head Luger. The skull over the chamber was cut deeply.

He returned the rag to the drawer and holstered the weapon. He always kept it very clean. And it had always served him well.

He went over to the window. It was snowing quite heavily now. He watched the snowflakes building on the sill.

And then, for a moment, he was once again in Russia.

Endless. Frozen. Always the terrible, terrible penetrating cold. Blitzkrieg. Armored units rolling night and day. Supply lines outdistanced. Winter gear hundreds of miles to the rear. The barbaric hordes. Always retreating. But never quite quitting.

Hands and feet. Heavy machine guns and engines. All frozen. Blanketwrapped boots. Unshaven. The Luger jumping in his hand. Even women and children. But they weren't like other women and children. You could give them bread. Even when there wasn't enough. And they would bury a knife in you. And strip your body of clothing and weapons. Even before you were dead.

There was a knock, and Scharenführer Meyer came into the room.

"Sturmmann Beck's transfer," he said.

Spaatz signed it. "The staggering schedule?"

"Working on it now, sir." Meyer clicked his heels, and went out again.

The Castle Klessheim. A nightmare for one charged

with security.

The Führer saw most people right here at the Berghof. But frequently, for one reason or another — courtesy, strategy, whatever — he would journey to Klessheim Castle.

A narrow mountain road. Trees. Boulders. Everything possible was anticipated, and there was possible danger at every turn. There was a "flying" patrol, and a slow moving, searching patrol. There was always a vehicle out in front of the Führer's motorcade, at the proper distance, in case of mines or bombs.

And there was always at least one car in front of, and one behind the Führer's, with handpicked bodyguards. The finest. All vehicles moving as fast as possible. All in radio contact. And the Führer's Mercedes-Benz was especially built.

But still . . .

Chapter 8

It was called the Lion's Head. It'd first opened its doors
in 1789. And since that time it'd been known as a quiet,
comfortable place where a man could have a pint, a
game, and a sociable chat. Until the summer of 1939.

After that, with the general mobilization, and the concentration of troops in the south of England, the at-
mosphere of the place had begun to change.

And now, early in 1944, with the Island literally creaking under the weight of Allied troops and the invasion
build-up, the Lion's Head had become a favorite water-
ing hole of the Yanks. The previous owners were obviously rolling over in their graves.

Percy Hastings and Philip Joubert stood at the bar sipping their whiskey. They were in civilian clothes. And
rather out of place, with the rest of the public house given
over to the boisterous crew of an American B-17 bomber
called "Waltzing Mathilda."

Meg, the rather buxom barmaid, came up and put her
arm around Hastings. "You two look like the gloom of
death," she said. "Look 'round. Maybe you should get
adventuresome and join up."

She was joking, of course. Though she didn't know exactly what they did, she had a pretty good idea. When
you've been with a man in the closest way you get to

know things about him, even when he doesn't tell you.

"We . . . lost a friend," said Hastings.

"Oh, Percy, I'm sorry to hear that."

"It's the times."

She nodded her agreement.

The two Americans standing next to them turned. From earlier conversation between themselves, easily overheard, the shorter one, a corporal, was a waist gunner. The other one, a sergeant, was a belly gunner. Both were very, very young, and both had shot down Messerschmitts that morning in a successful bombing run into the heart of Germany. They were feeling no pain.

"Hey, Percy," said the corporal.

Hastings ignored it. His first name'd been the start of things more than once.

"Oh Per-cy." The sergeant pitched his voice.

Hastings looked at them.

"I've got a question, Percy the civilian," said the corporal.

"Easy, my friend," said Joubert. "It's not the way you think."

"I'm not your friend, Frenchy," said the corporal. "Not his, either." He gestured around the room. "These are my friends."

Most of the bomber crew were watching them now, waiting for the coming fracas.

Except for the commander of the B-17. His thoughts were only for the blond on his lap. She was wearing his cap. And his hand was lost in the folds of her skirt.

"If you can't handle it, pack it out of here," said Meg.

"We can handle it all right," said the sergeant.

"What I want to know is this," said the corporal. "Why we risk our ass trying to pull your fuckin' chestnuts out of the fire, and you two stand here tonight drinking like men."

Joubert's hand went to his shirt collar, as though in a nervous gesture, and then started inside his coat.

"No," said Hastings. He knew the Frenchman was carrying a Fairbairn knife sheathed upside down beneath his armpit. And he wouldn't have been surprised at a Browning, either, though it was strictly against regulations. "We'll leave."

"Like hell you will," said the corporal. "You'll answer the question to my satisfaction, or I'm going to take your fuckin' head off."

Hastings sighed and eased Meg aside. He was wondering if he could just turn abruptly and walk out when the corporal made a mistake. He grabbed Hastings by the collar. "Take your hands off me, son."

The corporal blinked. If he hadn't had so much to drink he would have caught the danger in the quiet words. Instead, all he heard was the word "son," and that rankled his drunken anger all the more.

"I'm not going to ask you again," said Hastings. His instincts were to attack and keep on attacking. That'd been his training and his life for more than four years. The bridge of the nose to the base of the throat. Either side of the head and throat, from the temple to the base of the throat. The back of the neck, immediately on either side of the spine. "From now on, gents, avoid friendly fights," W.E. "Deacon" Fairbairn had told his group in the summer of 1940. "You'll likely kill your friend."

"You won't have to, you son of a bitch." The corporal came with a roundhouse swing.

Hastings easily parried the blow, and speared for the American's nose and eyes. At the last moment he chang-

61

ed the jab and struck the forehead soundly with the heel of his hand.

The corporal staggered back, tripped, and went down, disoriented.

The sergeant stepped in. He, too, was prone to the haymaker style of fighting. Hastings buried his fist in the man's belly. There was a whoosh of air. The sergeant slowly sat down, and then was quickly sick.

The Lion's Head was nearly silent for the better part of a minute. Then the melee was on. A PFC came charging at Joubert. The fat Frenchman deftly sidestepped and then kicked the airman's feet out from under him. The PFC slammed into the bar like a sack of flour thrown by a hefty stevedore. Ancient oak paneling cracked.

It went quickly. The Americans, though superior in number, were outclassed. Hastings and Joubert had been well trained in the art of hand-to-hand combat. They had that ability to watch a blow come, and then to do something about it before it landed.

The crew of the "Waltzing Mathilda," while no doubt competent at their profession, had obviously had their hand-fighting experience confined to the likes of the scrapping and boxing of their school days.

"That's enough, Gawd dammit!" The commander of the B-17, a first lieutenant, was on his feet, almost dumping the blonde to the floor. He, too, was young, but he had the mannerism of one who's been a leader for a long time.

The Lion's Head quieted.

He walked unsteadily over to Hastings. The girl followed. "That's just enough, you big bastard," he said. "I know they shouldn't have started in on you, but that's just enough." He looked at his watch. "We're back on alert in less than eight hours. You put one of them in the

62

hospital and I'll have your ass for breakfast. You read me, Mister?"

Hastings found himself nodding.

"I haven't missed a run yet, and I'm not about to start now, just because I can't muster a full crew." He took his cap from the girl, and put it on at a jaunty angle. "You just might find yourself taking their place. And I can guarantee you the flak's damned heavy where we go." With that, and without the slightest hint of a warning, he threw a punch at Hastings.

It was a harmless, glancing blow. But Hastings, who'd stepped back instinctively, slipped on some spilled whiskey and went down.

There was applause.

Without more ado, the lieutenant walked out of the Lion's Head, his arm around the blond. The crew of the "Waltzing Mathilda" followed.

Hastings got to his feet wiping blood from his lip.

"Are you all right?" asked Meg.

"I've hurt myself worse shaving."

The owner of the Lion's Head came warily in from the back room. "Coo blimey. Who's going to pay?"

Hastings took some bills from his pocket and gave them to him.

"That's not enough."

Meg gave him a look. "You make more in a week now than you did in a year before the war."

There was no arguing that. He frowned but he returned to his back room.

"You know something," said Hastings. "I feel better." He picked up Meg and put her over his shoulder, helping himself to a generous feel of her behind as he did so. She swatted at him, but missed. They started for the stairs.

"I can ring up Gladys for you," she called back.

63

"Thanks, no," said Joubert. He'd located a bottle of French wine and had poured a glass.

On the stairs there was whispering. And a throaty giggle.

Upstairs, a door opened and closed.

Then the sound of bed springs.

Joubert smiled. And raised his glass.

9

Lieutenant Colonel George Dalbert and Captain David Weinberg shared an antique upholstered bench in a vestibule in one wing of the White House. Both men were nervous, and both showed it.

Following the phone call from Fort Bliss, Dalbert had written a brief report regarding the proposed assassination of Chancellor Adolf Hitler. He'd recommended that a file be opened.

On his return to Washington, Weinberg had gone into more detail.

One day had passed. Then Major General John Stripe, liaison to the White House, called. Could they please come right over?

"Gentlemen."

They came to their feet.

"Stand easy." General Stripe had a boyish grin that was catching. He shook hands with them. "We have five minutes. Ten if necessary."

"Any advice?" asked Dalbert.

"Keep it simple. Shoot straight. All right? Let's go."

Franklin Delano Roosevelt looked up from the papers spread on his desk. The familiar smile. A cigarette holder clenched in his teeth. "George. David. Thank you for coming." He put a cigarette in the holder and lighted it.

"This Hitler thing. Can you do it?"

He doesn't mince words, thought Weinberg.

Dalbert cleared his throat. "It's possible, Mr. President. A lot of ifs."

"Fascinating," said Roosevelt. "Such a subtle distinction. Instead of an elaborate plan built around an anticipated movement or appearance, with all the inherent problems of timing and so forth . . . It's rather like having some people blend into the background at Hyde Park. Just waiting."

"Yes, sir," said Dalbert.

Roosevelt picked up some papers, but didn't really look at them. "What would be the absolute earliest that you could make the attempt?"

Dalbert and Weinberg looked at each other.

"A few weeks? By the first part of April?" He put the papers down again. "That could be very important."

The significance of that was not missed. Indeed, the whole world was waiting for the invasion of the continent of Europe from the west. That it was coming was not in doubt. The speculation went to just when and where.

"What do you think?" asked Dalbert.

Weinberg considered for a moment. "There's a German colonel at Bliss that looks good on paper," he said. "We haven't approached him yet, of course. And Major Patch seemed to have someone in mind for the fourth man."

"You'd be going in with the team?" asked Roosevelt.

"Yes, sir."

"He's personally acquainted with the Berchtesgaden area," said Dalbert.

"What about the inside man?" asked General Stripe. "The local citizen."

Weinberg shook his head.

"We have no one?" asked Roosevelt.

"No, sir," said Dalbert.

"The British?"

"I'm inclined to think they do. I had lunch with Brigadier Pound yesterday. Tried to feel him out a bit."

"Then we'll make it a joint venture. Use a couple of their people. That would be good policy anyway."

Like a warm knife through butter, thought Weinberg.

Roosevelt snubbed out his cigarette, and put the holder on the desk. The FDR of the newsreels. "Gentlemen, let's do it. Just as quickly as humanly possible."

The traffic on Pennsylvania Avenue was fairly heavy, notwithstanding the early afternoon hour. Uniforms were everywhere. Stripe, Dalbert, and Weinberg stood by a navy recruiting poster. A sunny spot, out of the wind.

"For now," said Stripe, "the authority for this mission is strictly OSS."

Dalbert and Weinberg looked at him. It'd been minutes since they'd left the White House.

"There hasn't been time to weigh the political implications," he said.

"Of going after a gangster . . . " started Dalbert.

"There's more to it than that," said Stripe. "The possibility of an embarrassing failure. At this time. The man's deserved place in history a century or two from now."

A redhead came out of a nearby shop, her back to them. Slender. Leggy. They watched until she turned into another store.

"Does that mean that General Blackford shouldn't be told of the President's . . . interest?" asked Dalbert. "I promised to keep him advised."

Stripe grinned. "If Thad knew FDR was backing this

67

he'd want to personally join the team. Be the first out of the plane. Parachute or not."

The redhead came out of the store, looked their way momentarily, and then walked on down the street.

Ugly as sin.

It was a small park. But they went there often. Just a couple of benches, a swing, and a teeter-totter. And a few large old trees. Rather somber now with their naked limbs and the gathering darkness.

Weinberg had gone home early. There'd been no reason not to. The westbound B-25 that he was hitching a ride on was leaving early the next morning. And that was all the time he had.

Ben and Sarah were listening to a radio serial when he got home. And Judith and he had slipped upstairs to the bedroom. He'd wanted to tell her then. But he didn't. It was a happy time.

They'd gone to a favorite delicatessen for hot pastrami sandwiches. And then across the street to the park.

A chill wind kicked up some leaves. Judith snuggled against him. Ben and Sarah squealed and raced to the teeter-totter.

For a long time neither spoke.

"Tell me," said Judith finally.

He looked at her.

"You're going away, aren't you?"

"Yes."

"Where?"

"England."

"And?"

"And."

"Oh God." Her fingers squeezed him.

He couldn't tell her he'd volunteered. At the moment

he didn't know why he had. There were others that were familiar with Berchtesgaden. Most spoke German. And there were even a few who'd also been professors of European history.

It'd had something to do with the uncle who'd raised him, taken him to Germany on occasion, and who'd never returned from a trip there back in 1937. But only partly so.

"How long do we have?" she asked.

"Tonight."

There was a bang, and Sarah began crying.

They hurried to her.

"Benny jumped off on purpose," she said.

"I kind of slipped off," Ben said, coming round to see if she was all right.

Weinberg picked her up. "It's getting too dark," he said.

They headed out of the park. Judith had her arm around him. And Ben had hold of his trench coat.

"I'm afraid," Judith said softly.

And, for the first time, so was he. This had to be the best of all possible worlds.

Dalbert and Milly had left the building at the same time. They'd gotten to talking. He'd picked up a paper. And in the rush-hour crowds they'd both missed their buses.

He'd suggested a drink at a nearby place. She'd agreed. And then they'd had another.

She was from Joplin, Missouri, but had been in the nation's capital since just before the war, and was totally enamored with it.

He told her about Des Moines, and the law practice he'd had there. And so the conversation had gone. Light. Comfortable.

Then, he just said it. "Milly, I want to make love to you."

A bit of a smile. She hardly hesitated. "All right."

At Dalbert's apartment passion flared quickly.

Milly slipped out of her clothes. A most beautiful woman. The pale skin a stark contrast to her black hair. Large breasts with flushed, erect nipples. Full hips. Deeply sensuous. She lay down on the plush living room rug. And invited him.

He hurriedly undressed. But what should have been, wasn't. Her eyes showed her disappointment.

He knelt and kissed her. Stroked her. Wanting her. But nothing.

After a while he went over to the window. "Maybe later . . . " There was a tightness in his voice.

She didn't answer.

He turned.

She'd put her clothes on.

"I'll see you . . . " he started.

"It's all right," she said. And she was gone.

He watched her get into a cab and drive away. And for a very long time he just stood at the window. Finally he picked up his clothes and put on a robe. There was still the faint smell of her presence.

He made some coffee, and wandered around the tiny apartment, restless. He found himself staring at a snapshot on the dresser. His wife and daughter, standing by the old hackberry tree. On a warm summer day.

He picked up the phone, and asked for the long-distance operator.

10

Sergeant Andrew Holt pulled the pin out of the hand grenade. The recruits sitting on the ground around him watched, closely, silently. They knew it was a live grenade. He had their attention.

He tossed the pin to a chubby, pink-faced boy on his left. Boy? He was probably older than Holt.

Holt glanced at him again. A boy nonetheless.

"The fuse isn't activated until you release this," said Holt, pointing. "Then you have five seconds. In an actual combat situation you'd probably want to give it a count or two. Otherwise you may get the damned thing thrown back at you. But that doesn't concern us here today.

"Just lob it. Don't see how far, or how hard you can throw it. Just lob it in the proximity of your target. And get your butt down." He looked around. "Any questions?"

A tall drink of water in the back raised his hand.

"Yes?"

"What would happen if you were to accidently drop that thing now, Sarge?" He had a deep voice.

Holt smiled. "Then you better hope I'm the kind of man that'll lay down across it."

There was some nervous laughter.

"I've seen it done," said Holt. "Anything else?" He

pointed to the chubby, pink-faced recruit. The name tag said Wilson. "All right, trooper, let's you and I go forward and throw this damned thing." He took the pin from him and put it back in the hand grenade.

They moved out around the protective mound of dirt to the waisthigh rectangle of sand bags. Some twenty-five yards or so distant there were several rubber tires that'd seen better days, on the hand grenade range as well as the road.

Holt handed him the grenade. "Just relax," he said. "Pull the pin, toss it, and get down."

Wilson gave him a grin. He pulled the pin, and then reared back to try and throw it a country mile.

But he'd turned the grenade in his hand. The fuse was armed.

"Throw it, soldier," said Holt. "Now!"

Wilson looked at him, and then at the grenade. And froze. The grenade rolled out of his hand to their feet.

Holt grabbed him by the jacket and flung himself over the sandbags, pulling the recruit with him.

The hand grenade exploded even before they'd hit the ground. Gravel rained across them.

After Holt'd made certain they were both all right he gave serious consideration to kicking Wilson's ass. But the recruit was hurting enough already. He had the shakes. And the once pink face was sickly pale.

Holt patted him on the back of the neck. "It's all right," he said.

A jeep with two officers in it was just pulling up when they same back around the mound of dirt. Wilson went over and sat down, kind of off by himself.

"Smoke if you've got 'em," said Holt, heading over to the jeep.

The two officers got out. The one was smiling.

"Well I'll be damned," said Holt. He and Patch shook hands.

"This is Dave Weinberg," said Patch. "Dave, Andy Holt."

Holt remembered himself and started to salute. But Weinberg held out his hand, and they shook hands.

"How've you been?" asked Patch.

"Can't complain, I guess," said Holt. "You?"

"Good."

There was that warmth that exists between two men who've looked death in the face together.

"I'd have been in touch sooner," said Patch, "but I didn't know you were at Bliss. Until I started looking for you."

"Looking for me?"

"We've got a little thing going."

Holt grinned. "And you want a volunteer."

"Something like that."

"It's dangerous," said Weinberg. "Behind the lines. That's about all we can tell you now."

"I'm your man," said Holt quickly.

Patch looked at him. "Sure? This looks pretty soft."

"I'm sure."

A second lieutenant came over. A ninety-day wonder. There were salutes.

"Something wrong here, Sergeant?" he asked.

"No, sir."

"Then we'd better get on with the training. We're behind schedule."

"No, sir," said Holt. "Respectfully, sir."

"What?"

"I quit, sir."

"You what?"

"I'm going back to the war, sir. Before one of these fuckin' recruits kills me." With that Holt climbed into the jeep.

Patch and Weinberg did likewise.

They drove off.

73

The second lieutenant stared after them. His whole day, at least, had just been ruined.

At the NCO cadre barracks Holt stretched out on his bunk.

Major Patch'd said they would be flying out at midnight if all went well. They had to see someone else.

And it only took minutes to turn in bedding and pack a duffel bag.

From habit he reached for the soiled, worn letter in his shirt pocket. But he left it. Hell, he knew what it said.

The letter'd caught up with him just after he came out of surgery for the second time.

A plump WAC nurse, a big-sister type, had read it to him. At least the first part. Then she'd mumbled "bitch," and tucked the letter under his pillow. She'd stroked his cheek for a long time before leaving him.

Then he'd read it. And he'd cried. The big tough combat veteran. And he'd cried like a baby.

The letter'd been written almost a month earlier. She hoped it found him well, she said. She hadn't heard from him in such a long time. Nobody had. His folks either.

She didn't know how to tell him. She'd been lonely, and she'd gone out with Homer Kennedy . She thought she was pregnant. They were going to be married. And she was so very, very sorry.

Mary Sue Hanley. By now Mary Sue Kennedy. Homer doing it to her every day. Two or three times a day. Her belly swelling. Holt wondered if that'd ever stop eating at him.

They'd gone steady since the beginning of their junior year. She'd been the homecoming queen. And he was captain of the football team.

People joke about making love in a haystack. But that

was where they'd first done it. She'd looked at him. He was too big for her, she'd said. That'd pleased him, but they'd quickly found out that such was not the case. They were going to get married. The first Sunday afternoon after graduation.

But Holt'd left for the army, receiving his high school diploma in absentia. And after only six weeks of basic infantry training he and thousands of others were rushed to the shores of North Africa.

Homer Kennedy. Probably two years older than Holt.

Old man Kennedy'd had the lumnber yard in Greenfield. And when the war clouds had started to gather he'd bought son Homer a small farm out east of town. A necessary occupation. And thus a draft deferment.

So he could stay home and fuck Mary Sue.

Holt got up, stripped his bunk, and folded the mattress.

Dangerous, the man'd said. Behind the lines. There was a tingle of excitement, of life. For the first time since he'd received the letter. That fuckin' letter.

"Quote. 'The only thing that would help my country would be for that raving madman in the Chancellory . . .' Unquote. Sentence unfinished. Quote. 'He is leading Germany into a deep, dark abyss from which it will never return. It's that simple.' Unquote." Weinberg handed the file to Patch. "Is that exact, Mrs. Adams?"

"Verbatim." She tapped the ash from her cigarette. "I won't ask what this is about. But you understand they frequently say what they think you want to hear."

Patch nodded. "What's your considered opinion?"

Constance Adams thought for a moment. "There've been so many." But she remembered him. Very well. "I believe he was sincere," she said.

75

"We'd like to talk to him," said Patch.

Standartenführer Max Wolff waited for the MP corporal to open the door for him, and then stepped into the interrogation room. The door closed softly behind him.

The room was painted a pale green, and had the spartan furnishings typical of so many military establishments.

The two American officers saluted.

He returned the salute, noting the file on the table. They had more than a passing interest in him.

There were introductions.

"Patch," he said. "An unusual name."

The major smiled. "My parents started through immigration named Patchowski, and came out Patch."

"They didn't mind?"

"They thought it rather suited their new image as Americans."

"That's interesting."

"Any interest in Jewish names?" asked the captain, pleasantly enough.

Wolff glanced at Weinberg. "Not really," he said, returning his attention to the major. His first impressions were seldom wrong. He rather liked the major, but not necessarily the captain.

Patch handed him three packs of cigarettes. "The lady said you were partial to Lucky Strikes."

He took them, pocketed two, and opened the other. "Please thank Frau Adams." He took his time lighting up, wondering just what they wanted. He inhaled deeply and let it out slowly. How could anything that tasted so good be bad for you?

"I'll lay it on the line," said Patch. "We want you to help us kill Adolf Hitler."

There was a most pregnant silence.

Then Wolff smiled. "For three packs of Lucky Strikes? That would have to make me the most underpaid assassin in history."

They smiled briefly at his humor.

"But then you're serious, aren't you?"

"Forgive the play on words," said Weinberg. "Deadly serious."

Again, a pause.

"You're asking me to personally assist you . . . "

"Yes," said Patch.

It was like a bolt of lightning out of a clear sky. Wolff's mind raced. Whatever the scheme, it had to take them to the Continent, to Germany. But he mustn't appear anxious. "Why would I do such a thing?"

Weinberg tapped the file on the table. "For the world, Standartenführer Wolff," he said. "For your country, as well as ours."

Wolff nodded slowly. "When? Where?"

"Obviously we're not going to tell you that," said Patch. "Maybe later. When we're close."

"Do I have a choice?"

"You do. But you'll be put in isolation until it's over. That may be a long time."

"I don't think I would like that."

"When it's finished," said Patch, "when I give the word — or Captain Weinberg here — you can either stay with us, or take a walk."

Wolff was looking at his cigarette, but he was listening very closely.

"But if you try and go over the hill before then—take French leave or whatever the hell you people call it — I'll put a .45 round in the back of your head. In case that crossed your mind."

Wolff took a last pull on the cigarette and stubbed it

out. "That should be a nine-millimeter round, Major. That clumsy Colt automatic you Americans are so fond of would be rather conspicious where you're going. Where we're going, I should say."

11

A blue '40 Ford convertible pulled to the curb, its windshield wipers beating a steady rhythm against the light rain. The driver moved over. A man in a trenchcoat got in behind the wheel.

For a long moment Patch and Adele Blackford just looked at each other. There was that shyness that comes with not being with a person for a long time. But there were memories, too.

He took her in his arms and kissed her. Gently at first. Then harder. She returned his passion.

Finally they parted, reluctantly.

He turned up the heater.

"Did I keep you waiting long?" she asked.

"Not long."

"Miserable night."

"Depends how you look at it." He patted her thigh. She smiled.

Soon they were headed into downtown El Paso. Not far from the Mexican border they turned onto a side street.

In the lobby of the La Grande Hotel Adele found a framed picture of some fruit on the far wall to study while Patch checked in. Mr. and Mrs. John Smith. Chicago. Then he noticed that the third line up on the register had a John Smith and wife, of Dallas. He smiled. Common name.

The dried-up hotel clerk seemed not to notice. He smelled of Muscatel. "Luggage?"

"It's on its way," said Patch.

The clerk handed over the key. "Second floor. Third on the left."

The room had once been a bright, and probably cheerful yellow. Now it was faded and peeling. The naked, overhead bulb seemed to accent the shabbiness of the tired furniture.

The radiator hissed and popped.

"You pick the damn'dest romantic places," said Adele. She was obviously a bit nervous, and thus a bit irritable.

Patch smiled. "You said someplace out of the way."

"This is so damned far out of the way . . . I'm sorry."

"Bed looks comfortable."

"It does, doesn't it."

He took out a small bottle of whiskey, poured a bottom-full into a water glass, and handed it to her.

She sipped, made a face, and handed it back. "Why is it," she asked, "every so often we come back into each other's lives? To hurt each other."

He drained the glass, and put it on the dresser. "Love."

"Is it?"

"Isn't it?"

"You know, Patch, I do love you."

"Then . . . "

"But nothing's changed."

He reached for her.

She came closer.

He began to undress her. Her smallness, and his need, made him feel strong, almost powerful.

"Turn off the light." She began unbuckling his belt.

"I want to see you."

They turned off the overhead light, and left the bathroom light on.

They made love with an urgency born of the times. For there was no tomorrow. And while such is always true, somehow it was more true at that moment.

There was a fire in each that had been waiting for a very long time. Each took. And each gave.

And there was love. Of the highest form. That can be experienced in no other way.

The cockpit window of the C-47 slid open. The pilot stuck his head out into the drizzle. "Clear!" he yelled.

There was a whine as the number one engine began to crank. Then a sputter and a cough, and the noisy, powerful engine came to life. The starboard engine followed suit.

The plane began to taxi, and the runway lights came on. It turned onto a main runway, into the wind, and hesitated.

Then came the clearance. Full throttles. The engines roared. The plane began to move, slowly at first, then faster and faster. The tail came up. Then it was airborne, its gear going up. And it was gone. Into the wet, inky night.

Adele wondered whether it was her, or whether she'd actually seen him wave.

She wondered, too, where he and the others were going. He hadn't said. But he'd seemed excited about it. She turned from the fence and started for the parking lot.

She pushed a strand of hair from her face. Between the rain and the lovemaking her hair was a mess. She smiled. The La Grande Hotel. But it'd been good. Very good. It seemed so far away now. Almost like a dream.

She stepped in an ankle-deep puddle of water as she passed an enclosed jeep. "Damn," she mumbled under her breath. Then she heard the canvas covered door of the jeep open. She started walking faster.

"Adele?"

She stopped. There was no mistaking the voice. She started back. Her husband stepped out of the jeep. All six-foot four of him.

On the other side, PFC Mullins climbed out. "Evening, Ma'am."

"Good evening."

"What are you doing here?" Blackford's tone was cordial, not betraying the suspicions that were probably there.

She felt numb. She cared. But she didn't. It made a difference. And yet it didn't. Life was a habit. And it took guts to change it. "Looking for you."

"Me? But how could you know I was here?" The logical professional, and the suspicions were surfacing now. There was silence. She had no answer. Perhaps it was just as well.

"I told her, sir."

They both looked at Mullins.

"She called just as we were leaving the office, sir. I told her we'd probably be here later seeing some people off. I guess I forgot to tell you."

"Yes you did." Blackford turned to Adele. "What . . ."

She shrugged. The soggy strand of hair'd slid back across her face. "I just thought we'd have some middle-of-the-night ham and eggs somewhere like we used to."

Blackford smiled. He seemed genuinely pleased. "I'll be with Mrs. Blackford," he told Mullins, returning the salute almost before it was given.

In the car he leaned over for what Adele thought would be his customary hello-kiss on the cheek. Instead he kissed her full on the mouth, and with more than a little passion. His hand rested on her knee.

"Whiskey?"

She had to think for a moment, and then remembered. "A toddy. The rain. I'm catching cold."

"Oh." He ran his hand up her dress, to the softness of her thigh.

She put her hand on his to stop him. It was totally unlike him. "This will never do," she said in a light, teasing voice. "The General and his lady . . . in a parking lot."

He laughed softly. "You're absolutely right." He squeezed her thigh and sat back. "Think you could get along without me for a while?"

She looked at him.

He had the beaming look of a schoolboy who's just been selected captain of his basketball team *and* who's also received the top report card. "I've been assigned to Ike's staff."

"Oh, Thad, that's wonderful." She moved close to him, her hand on his shoulder. "When . . . "

"This afternoon. I'm to report at the earliest convenience. Which'll be damned quick, I can assure you. It'll mean another star, and who knows . . . "

"Oh Thad, I'm so happy for you."

He was grinning, no longer the general, the professional. "Let's skip the ham and eggs . . . "

There was a heaviness in her throat. She knew it was guilt. "I'm yours to command, General."

"That's my gal." He started the car.

Soon they were on Artillery Avenue, headed for home.

"Hello?" said the sleep-filled voice.

"Hello," said Mullins.

"Do you know what time it is?"

"That's the first thing you say to me?"

"I didn't say I wasn't glad to hear from you. I just asked if you knew what time it is."

"Yeah, I know what time it is." He wiggled his toes. The telephone booth was cold.

"So how are you?" she asked.

"All right. You?"

"All right." There was a pause. "I'd be better if you'd stop playing soldier and come home."

"This isn't something you just quit . . . "

"I bet if I told some people just how old you are . . . "

"Don't do that." His voice was a bit sharp, and then softened. "This is something I need, Flo."

"I know. I was just kidding."

"So how's the place doing?"

"We're getting rich. You should be here."

"I miss you."

"I miss you, too." She lowered her voice. "My backside gets cold at night without you."

"So get a hot water bottle."

She snorted. "Next time you're home and want to start fooling around, I'll tell you . . . "

He laughed.

The operator came on the line. "Your time is up."

"I'll be talking to you," he said.

"Take care of yourself."

They hung up.

And along with thousands of others at Fort Bliss that night Mullins was a very lonely soldier.

12

Willi stood by the heavy, red velvet curtain that separated the large living room from the famous picture-window room. Attentive. Available. And largely unnoticed. Which was as it should be.

It was his first day at the Berghof. And he was now Rottenführer Willi Roehrs. He forced back a smile. He was pleased with himself. And with the new work, too. At least so far.

He'd been given a tour that morning by one of the older secretaries. They'd started on the second floor, where the Führer lived. There'd been deadly silence, since he still slept. In front of one door there'd been two black Scotch terriers, Eva Braun's dogs, Stasi and Negus. Next'd come Hitler's bedroom. The two rooms, it seemed, were connected by a large bathroom. The walls of the hallway were decorated with exotic vases, beautiful pieces of sculpture, and paintings by the old masters. It was all very fine, but there was also something strange and impersonal about it.

And with the living room here, too, thought Willi. Despite the thick carpets and beautiful Gobelins. I've been too long in the barracks, he decided.

And that was it. The Führer was basically a plain and simple man. He'd once been a corporal, too. And he'd never forgotten it.

The guests talked quietly. And waited. It was nearly 4:00 P.M. Most of them had been waiting for some time now. Suddenly a hush spread over the room. The noon briefing was over.

Chancellor Adolf Hitler entered the room.

A tingle danced up Willi's spine. It was the closest he'd ever been.

The Führer seemed tired. And a bit stooped. It was because of the heavy burdens he carried, he'd once said.

Then, almost as if by signal, Eva Braun made her appearance, accompanied by the two scampering dogs.

"The Lady at the Berghof."

Willi'd been part of the bodyguard on several of her skiing outings. He'd found her pleasant, though he'd heard she was openly ignored and snubbed by the wives of Göring, Goebbels, and Ribbentrop.

Hitler kissed her hand, and then greeted each guest with a handshake. It was the transformation of a man of state burdened by the tragedies of battle to the jovial host, eager to please guests and helpmate.

The men addressed Eva with a slight bow. "Gnädiges Fraulein."

Eva and the other women began talking fashion.

Finally Hitler interrupted, chuckling. He pointed to the two dogs. "Hand-sweepers," he said.

There was good-natured laughter.

Eva retorted that Hitler's dog, Blondi, was a calf.

There was more laughter, with Hitler obviously enjoying the familiar bantering.

The pleasantries over, Hitler selected the buxom wife of a Krupp Works' industrialist and escorted her to the table.

They were followed by Martin Bormann and Eva.

Most knew of Eva's dislike for the stocky Bormann,

mainly because of his flagrant philandering. Except for Eva herself of course, anything in skirts was his target. And this with an attractive, but permanently pregnant wife.

A cart was wheeled in by a mess steward.

The Hauptscharenfuhrer removed the lid from a silver service, took a small amount on a spoon, and handed it to Willi.

Willi tasted, smiled slightly, and nodded. It was terrible. Baked potato soaked in raw linseed oil.

The distinction of tasting went to the new man. A dubious distinction. Not that there was any real concern over poisoning. All of the Führer's meals were prepared under the supervision of the SS in the Berchtesgaden clinic of Dr. Werner Zabel, brought up to the Berghof, and warmed. It was just that most of what the Fuhrer ate wasn't very appealing.

The Hauptscharenführer served the Führer. Willi and another Rottenführer served the others. Sauerbraten. The aroma was fantastic. Now that was Willi's idea of a real meal.

Hitler began speaking of vegetarianism. He told of a slaughterhouse he'd visited in the Ukraine. Work girls in rubber boots. Blood up to their ankles. Several guests blanched. One stopped eating altogether.

There was a knowing glint of amusement in Hitler's eyes. Abruptly he began charming his guests with tales of his youth.

Willi was spellbound, until he caught the signal from the Hauptscharenführer. He began refilling the guests' waterglasses.

Eva mentioned some plays and movies.

"I cannot watch a film," said Hitler, "while the people are making so many sacrifices. Besides, I must save my eyes for studying maps and reading frontline reports."

Again, the tiredness showed.

Willi had just finished filling Martin Bormann's glass, and was returning it to the table.

"Mein Führer . . ." Bormann gestured with his hand. And knocked the glass from Willi's grasp. With a deft movement Willi caught the glass before it struck the floor. But not before its contents were spilled on the Reichsleiter's lap.

There was a momentary silence. The Hauptscharen-führer was quickly upon them, dabbing with a napkin.

The Führer's look was one of understanding. It was all right. Conversation continued. But was it all right?

There'd also been a look from Bormann. Just a quick one. And it'd chilled Willi.

"Did he say anything?" asked Hannah.

"Not then. Not later."

"Then . . ."

"Maybe," said Willi.

They were sitting at the oak table in Hannah's kitchen sharing a bottle of beer and a large, soft pretzel liberally dabbed with hot mustard.

She pinched off a bit of the pretzel and popped it in his mouth.

He smiled. "After lunch we all went to the tea house. Maybe a twenty-minute's walk. You'd love the view. The Ach River roaring down the mountainside. The towers of Salzburg."

"Sounds beautiful."

"It is." He offered her the bottle of beer.

She declined.

He drained it and set it aside. He took her hand. The familiar look.

She feigned surprise. "Are you going to be this attentive after we're married?"

"More so."

"Then I think I'm going to like marriage." She began unbuttoning her blouse. Just far enough.

"Witch."

She had him off guard with her teasing. But she could tell he liked it, too.

She stood, and gave him a little bump with her behind as she went past.

She started for the bedroom, walking slow, letting her hips roll full. "I'm not bashful about the things I like, Willi." He was still worried. And all over a stupid glass of water.

Scharenführer Meyer swiveled his chair back and forth. It squeaked. But only when he swiveled left. And not right. He wondered about that.

He was alone.

Haupsturmführer Spaatz was on another inspection tour on the road to Klessheim Castle. A security-conscious devil, that one. But then that was why he was in charge.

The guard was posted. The morning report was finished. The orders of the day were complete. And all problems, great and small, were resolved. At least for the moment.

And Meyer had nothing to do. But he dare not leave, or otherwise indulge himself. Spaatz would have his head. Perhaps literally.

He glanced around. And then went quickly into his bottom desk drawer. He came out with a pickled egg, wolfed it down, and resumed swiveling.

He loved pickled eggs. For that matter he loved dark beer and fat Fräuleins. The one in frequent moderation.

And the other on occasion, when needed. But pickled eggs were simpler — and less expensive.

And Willi's Hannah could pickle an egg with the best of them.

He wondered again whether there was any connection between Hannah Müller and the Müller he'd known in Munich. Probably not. He hoped not.

Otto Müller. They'd been friends. They'd both fought in the Great War. Though not together.

They'd met afterwards in a bread line. In what was left of their Germany. Both were seeking work. And both were seeking . . . that something . . . for the years they'd spent in the trenches.

By some hand of fate, every few months, or years, their paths crossed. They would drink some beer, and talk far into the night. And then go their separate ways again.

Time passed.

Meyer found his place in the Schutzstaffel. And Müller rose steadily in the growing ranks of the Storm Troopers.

Then came that fateful day of June 30, 1934.

Thinking back on it, Meyer wasn't sure how much he'd known at the time, and what he'd learned later. There'd been much confusion.

Suddenly the word had come down. There was mutiny, rebellion, and high treason abroad in the land. The Storm Troopers. And others. Only the elite SS could be trusted.

For some time Ernst Röhm and his Storm Troopers had been agitating for more power, to become a people's army, to absorb the Reichswehr. Of course the Reichswehr would have none of it. There were too many brawlers and troublemakers in the ranks of the Storm Troopers. And rearmament was too serious a proposition.

Now, apparently, the Storm Troopers had gone too far.

At dawn the Führer himself had led a detachment of SS to the resort of Bad Wiesee, where he'd arrested Ernst Röhm. All over Germany there were arrests. And executions. General von Schleicher. Gustav von Kahr. Others.

Meyer's superior ordered him and another to proceed with haste to a nearby third-floor apartment. ". . . to bring in Lieutenant Otto Müller, one way or another." The implication was neither veiled, nor was it meant to be.

"Otto Müller?" Meyer questioned the orders. One of the few times in his life.

And he was reprimanded. Also one of the few times in his life.

The apartment was above the Old Strickmann restaurant, on a narrow side street near Munich's central business district.

Fritz, a young lad from Thuringia, and Meyer's companion for the arrest, was nervous. And he showed it. He pulled his revolver as soon as they started up the stairs.

"That's not necessary," said Meyer. "I know him." He noticed he hadn't called Müller his friend. Neither then nor back at headquarters.

Fritz returned the revolver to his pocket, but kept his hand on the butt.

At first there was no answer to Meyer's knock. He hammered on the door again.

"Who?"

"Meyer."

"It's open."

They entered.

Müller was sitting as his kitchen table. A lean, powerful man. "So what brings you . . ." The start of a smile faded. Fritz. The hand in the pocket. The meaning of the visit was apparent.

On the table in front of him there was a loaded magazine, and the butt assembly of a military Luger. The barrel assembly was in his hand. He'd been wiping it with a rag.

"We have to take you in," said Meyer. "I'm sorry. I'm sure it's some kind of misunderstanding."

"No," said Müller. "It's no misunderstanding." He slid the barrel assembly of the Luger back onto the butt.

"Don't do that," said Fritz, pulling his revolver.

Meyer took the revolver from him and put it in his pocket.

"All revolutions devour their own children," said Müller. "Did you know that? I read that somewhere. He needed us. Now he doesn't. Now he wants to be respectable." He put the loaded magazine into the butt of the Luger.

Fritz paled.

"Let me go," said Müller. "Let me make a run for it."

"I can't do that," said Meyer. "You know I can't."

"Then better here, than murdered behind bars, like some kind of animal."

"It won't be like that."

"That's right. It won't." Müller worked the toggle and charged the chamber. The muzzle started toward them.

"For God's sakes," screamed Fritz.

Meyer pulled his Walther, and shot Müller through the heart.

There'd been little investigation afterwards. Meyer'd been quickly absolved. And the matter quickly forgotten.

But Meyer remembered. The strange silence in the apartment afterwards. Nothing more than the contrast with a gun going off in a small room. But strange

92

nevertheless. An unreal feeling. But it was real. A man lay dead on the floor.

Otto Müller.

They'd been friends.

And those'd been bad times in Germany.

Outside, there was the sound of a motorcycle. Meyer stopped swiveling. Through the frosted pane he could see Hauptsturmführer Spaatz climbing out of the sidecar.

There'd be work enough now.

13

Captain Alistair Travis. At little more than five feet tall, with a slight build and the metal rimmed glasses, the first consideration was that the British army was now accepting all comers.

But there was something, his manner of walk, which was closer to a strut, that suggested that he was not quite what he first appeared. Or, more accurately, that there was more about him than there seemed to be.

Indeed, one was reminded of the ninety-pound weakling who's had sand kicked in his face at the beach by the bully. He's enrolled in the Charles Atlas body-building course. And flunked. And still picked up a trick or two along the way.

He looked at the motley group assembled in front of him. My God. Of all the missions he'd put together — coordinated was the word — this had to be the most unlikely. The big, strapping British sergeant-major, and the rough-looking American major excepted.

An obese Frenchman. And a scar-faced Nazi SS Colonel. My God. Who in the bloody hell had let those two sit next to each other? You could feel the sparks. They'd likely be at blows at any moment. Or worse.

But then if they were going on a mission together . . .

And Travis wasn't sure just what a Jew was supposed

to look like. But he'd give up lemon in his tea permanently if the American captain wasn't a Jew. And there was no love lost between him and the Nazi either.

My God.

The American sergeant would probably be all right. If the way he carried himself and the ribbons meant anything. Though he was little more than a schoolboy.

Well, a fair share of schoolboys had passed this way, too.

"Good morning, gentlemen," he said. "I'm Alistair Travis. I'm a captain. And more than a few have questioned the intelligence of that move."

A smile or two.

"It's my lot to help put these little sorties together. To do what I can for you. Maybe keep you alive an extra hour or two."

He waved a piece of paper. Underlining, circles, stamps, initials, signatures. Some in red.

"Signed by the PM himself. It says I'm to give you every possible assistance. Short of making my wife and my spinster sister available."

A bit of laughter.

"But then with the PM's signature . . . " Travis smiled. "Would any of you be interested in my sister? A bloody good cook. But then at forty-seven she's had a lot of time to practice."

More laughter.

The truth was, his sister was twenty-seven, attractive, and she couldn't boil water.

He turned serious. "Have any of you ever jumped out of an airplane?"

The hands went up. All of them.

Travis nodded. His biggest problem was out of the way. "More than the basic familiarization jumps?"

The Nazi, the Frenchman, and the British sergeant-major.

He pointed.

"Thirteen, sir," said the sergeant-major. "Six combat jumps."

"Seven," said the Frenchman.

You wouldn't have thought it.

The Nazi colonel smiled slightly. "One hundred and thirty-nine parachute jumps."

Travis looked at the floor for a moment. "Free-fall?"

"Yes."

"High-altitude, low-open?"

"Yes."

"Low-altitude?"

"Yes."

Travis shook his head and smiled. "We've instructors with less experience."

"So've we."

For a few seconds he studied the German. You didn't have to like him to admire him just a bit. "They haven't given me much time," he said. "Just until the next bomb run goes your way. So we'll be cramming a bloody lot into each and every hour.

"We'll be working off the tower with the harness. One of the worst things that can happen is a sprain or break going in. Have you all had combat experience?"

All but the Jewish captain.

"We'll be going through what you Yanks call the infiltration course. Live machine guns. Powder charges. That sort of thing. The confidence course. Climbing ropes and all that. Familiarization with German small arms.

"And then there'll be the little things. The little things that are probably the most important. If I catch one of you Yanks at the dinner table with other than a fork in

96

your left hand and the knife in your right I'll swat your hand just short of breaking your fingers."

Travis walked over to the Nazi colonel. He abruptly snatched a cigarette from the German's mouth and threw it across the room. His hand went into the tunic and came out with a pack of Lucky Strikes. He squeezed them. "That alone could have blown it."

Though outwardly calm, you could see in the German's eyes that he was bristling.

Travis dropped the crumpled pack of cigarettes in his lap and strutted off. "In short, gentlemen, I'm going to work your bloody ass off. And for every hour I have you you're going to be a better man for it." He gave the Frenchman a knowing glance.

"And when it's time, I'm going to buy each of you a pint. I'll shake your hand. And wish you Godspeed.

"And for those of you that make it back . . . well, you'll owe me a drink." He looked each in the eye, in turn.

"Now there's probably one or two of you that are wondering just where the hell that little martinet gets off. What are his qualifications?"

A smile or two. They sure as the hell were.

"Well, perhaps not all that much. I've helped send a lot of good people on their way. And I've gone myself three times." He paused for effect. "And most important . . . for you . . . I've come back three times."

It was almost dusk when it happened. It'd been one of those bone-chilling, gloomy days that England is famous, or rather infamous, for.

Travis had been pushing them hard since long before dawn. And they were tired. Jesus, they were tired. Almost to the point of being able to fall asleep on their feet.

P.U.–D

Tempers were short, but held in check. They were quiet, like men are when their bodies are pushed close to the limit of endurance, and who know what they're doing is necessary.

"You're dragging, gentlemen," said Travis. "Did you know that?"

No one answered.

"Do you know what it means when you're dragging?"

Still no answer.

"It means you lack confidence." He smiled. "And that calls for another dash through the confidence course, doesn't it?"

It would be easy to be violently pissed at the little captain, were it not for the fact that he'd done everything they'd done that day. And he still appeared reasonably fresh.

"This time with vigor, gentlemen." He held up his hand, something like a nineteenth century cavalry officer, yelled "Ho," and took off at a run.

They followed.

The leap across the trash pits.

Joubert had missed three times that day. Weinberg once. It was better if you cleared the pits.

This time they all did.

Then came the hand over-hand climb up the free-hanging rope.

Travis went up like a cat.

Slightly ahead of the rest, Joubert was next. Probably because his pride had been a bit wounded by the British captain.

Wolff was on his heels.

At something over twenty feet in the air Joubert slipped and slid, "burning" the rope with his hands. He struck Wolff, breaking the Nazi colonel's grasp.

Wolff had the choice of going into those below him, or pushing away, letting go altogether. He pushed away.

Joubert had the same choice and made the same decision. -

They landed in a heap together. And they came up swinging.

Then they backed off from each other slightly. And the real fight began.

Wolff made a quick sideways movement and kicked, catching the Frenchman painfully on the buttocks, almost putting him down.

And then the knife was in Joubert's hand. "Now taste cold steel," he said softly, a cruel smile on his face, and probably bitter memories in his heart.

Wolff whipped the wool scarf from his neck. Never taking his eyes off the Frenchman he wrapped his left hand and arm.

On the platform at the top of the rope climb Travis had watched for a moment, and then quickly started back down. The others, too, had stopped climbing, hesitated, and then scrambled for the ground.

The two combatants were circling. Joubert was making little jabs with the knife, feeling the German out, obviously aware that even though he was unarmed he was still a formidable opponent.

Patch came up behind Wolff, reached under the German's arms, then locked his wrists behind the neck, and lifted.

Hastings grabbed Joubert in a bear hug.

And it was over.

No it wasn't.

Joubert pulled free and lunged for the helpless Wolff. Weinberg stepped in, trying for the knife hand. He missed, and he paid for it. His arm was quickly bloody.

And it was definitely over.

Joubert looked at the knife, and at Weinberg. He made an apologetic gesture. "I'm sorry," he said.

Weinberg nodded.

From somewhere Travis came up with a first-aid kit and began working on Weinberg's arm. "Not too bad," he said. "A stitch or two, I'd say."

Weinberg and Wolff glanced at each other.

There was something of a smile in the Nazi colonel's eyes. In its way a "thank you."

"I think we'll call it a day," said Travis.

"Just one God damn minute," said Patch. He hadn't raised his voice, but the anger showed. "You two. The rest of you, for that matter. I don't give one damn what you sons of bitches do on your own time. But this is my time. From now until it's over. This horseshit jeopardizes the mission and every man on it. It happens again, and we're under way . . . you're a dead man. That I promise." He looked at Joubert. "You got it out of your system?"

The Frenchman was looking at the ground. He nodded.

Patch turned to Wolff. "You? Maybe you want more. Why don't you try me? Right here and now."

And I was right, Travis was thinking. A professional, and he isn't bluffing.

"No, Major," Wolff said finally. Not fear. Respect. "I think not."

14

Blackford trotted briskly up the stone steps. At the top the two armed sentries came to attention and saluted. Blackford returned the salute.

One of the sentries checked his identification, and then the other opened the door for him.

In the entranceway Blackford glanced at himself in the mirror that was provided for that very purpose. Everything was parade-ground perfect. From the gleaming combat boots, to the gleaming helmet that was now under his left arm, to the gleaming holster, which held the Colt .380 automatic pistol that was issued to general officers only. And there were fleeting memories of his days as a shavetail.

In the high-ceilinged reception room a paunchy major brought himself to attention in a relaxed, comfortable way, and saluted. He probably addressed superior officers every few minutes of every working day. "Good morning, General Blackford. Nice to see you, sir."

"Good morning," said Blackford, returning the salute. He was certain he'd never seen the man before.

"The General is expecting you, sir. If you'd just come this way."

They went down a hall, past a checkpoint and several armed sentries, to a large double door. The major opened the one for Blackford, and then closed it behind him.

Blackford threw a stiff salute and held it. "Brigadier General Thadeous W. Blackford reporting as ordered, *sir*."

The whole world was familiar with the warm smile of the man who called Abilene, Kansas, home. He quickly returned the salute, and then leaned across the large desk to shake hands. "Thad, you don't know how pleased I am that you're here."

"Thank you, sir."

"How's Adele? The family?"

"Just fine, sir. She sends her best. Mrs. Eisenhower?"

He tapped a letter on the desk. "Wants me to hurry up and get the war over with."

Blackford nodded, smiling.

"Well, Thad, I guess we'd better put you to work, hadn't we."

"I'm looking forward to it, sir."

Ike drew the curtain that was behind the desk. A full-wall map of England, the channel, and much of Europe.

Blackford stepped closer, savoring the challenge that was Eisenhower's, and that was now, to a lesser extent, his also.

"They know we're coming," said Ike. "There's certainly no secret about that."

Blackford ran a finger along the French coastline, noting troop positions.

"I just hope to God they don't know where." Ike pointed with a swagger stick. "There's the 'where.' "

"Normandy?"

"For a lot of reasons. You'll be fully briefed."

"The troop concentration's the lightest there," said Blackford. "For the moment, at least."

"For the moment."

Blackford looked at Ike. "A diversion?"

Ike's approval showed. "Exactly. And that's what you'll be doing with George Patton's First Army Group. Operation Fortitude."

Outside, Blackford climbed into the waiting jeep. On the road map he showed PFC Mullins the route to Kent. As the jeep pulled into traffic Blackford settled back to think.

In the back seat Major Willis cleared his throat quietly, but asked no questions.

Finally, Blackford turned. "George Patton's First Army Group. Kent."

Willis seemed puzzled. "But I thought . . . "

"That George was in hot water again? That's the scuttlebutt." And a general that's in trouble isn't given a battle command. Even if he is one of the finest fighting generals on the face of the earth. Blackford smiled. "If I know that old war horse we'll end up where the shooting is. No matter what."

At the First Army Group Headquarters in Kent, they passed through checkpoint after checkpoint. Their identification was checked, double-checked, and then confirmed by telephone.

There was an expectancy in the air.

Soldiers and equipment were everywhere around the hutted encampment. Or so it seemed at first.

"A God damn phantom army, Thad." Silver haired. Ramrod straight. A legend in his own time.

George Smith Patton. He was wearing cavalry boots, and a Colt Peacemaker. And there were probably other handguns secreted on him.

"Because the Germans respect me." He pointed out the window.

A corporal in a fatigue jacket and helmet-liner went into a nearby hut. Moments later he came back out. Minus the fatigue jacket. An overseas cap instead of the helmet-liner. And this time he was a PFC. You'd almost have to be inside the camp to pick up on it.

Patton pulled the shade. "We've got bogus radio traffic going out of here twenty-four hours a day, Thad. Troop movements. Supply movements. Anything to indicate a quick, heavy build-up."

He took a dust cover off a tablemap. The white bull terrier removed to the far side of the room to resume a nap.

"If you didn't know about Overlord and Normandy, where's the logical place to hit the Continent?"

"The Calais area," said Blackford. "Across the Straits of Dover. It's the closest . . . "

"And that's exactly what the German High Command has thought since 1942."

"The Fifteenth Army sector," said Blackford. "A crack outfit?"

"Hell, I haven't run into a pushover yet. But to answer your question, yes. One of the best."

Patton covered the map. "So that's our job, Thad. Operation Fortitude. Anything we can do to keep them thinking we're coming the obvious route. Perhaps as early as the first of May. Keep their reserves uncommitted and guessing."

He opened the shade. "But those sons of bitches aren't stupid. We've got to make them scratch for intelligence."

He got a faraway look in his eye. "If they find out about Normandy, Thad . . . God help those poor bastards if they get caught on the beaches."

"Then he said, 'For my part, my dog and I are seen

104

constantly around here. I give little talks to garden clubs.' " Blackford smiled. "Then he looked me straight in the eye and said, 'Isn't that a hell of a note?' "

Major Willis laughed.

Never one to waste time, Patton'd quickly seen them settled into a nearby office.

Blackford turned suddenly serious. "I just had a thought. Follow me through on it."

Willis nodded.

"You remember our little assassination plot from Bliss?"

"Of course."

"What do you think the chances are?"

"A snowball in hell. I've thought that from the start."

"They'll probably be captured, won't they? At least some of them."

"Yes, sir."

"They'll be interrogated."

"That's a kind word for it."

"They'll talk."

"Probably."

"And if they'd inadvertently learned something — something they weren't supposed to know — they'd divulge it, wouldn't they?"

"I'm not sure I follow you, sir."

"Find out if they're still in England."

15

Hannah Müller looked down from the hayloft, studying the area below.

Nothing.

But there'd been something . . .

Slowly, quietly, she descended the steep stairs.

There it was again. Almost imperceptible. But there was something . . . someone . . .

She quietly slipped the safety on the long-barreled artillery Luger.

She moved slowly across the barn, keeping the stalls as much as possible between her and the door to the kitchen.

At the door she stood to one side. Waiting. Listening.

Her imagination?

Probably.

But maybe not.

She eased the door open. Her finger trembled against the trigger.

She stepped into the kitchen, half expecting to see someone.

But nothing. Silence.

Suddenly the bedroom door opened.

The Luger exploded.

He had a surprised, silly grin on his face.

"Willi! *Mein Gott!*"

He slowly raised his hands, looked at the hole in the wall just to his left, and then at her. "Does that mean you don't want to make love?"

Half laughing and half crying she rushed to him and put her arms around him. "Are you all right?"

He took the Luger from her, returned it to safety, and put it on the chair.

"You aren't supposed to be here."

"I exchanged. I work tonight."

"But I didn't hear you."

"That woodcutter up the road. I caught a ride on his cart. I looked everywhere . . . "

"I could have killed you."

He began to caress her behind.

"*Mein Gott, Willi.* Is that all you ever think of?"

"But of course."

The olive drab three-quarter ton Dodge turned off the paved road onto a tree-lined lane. Ahead, the hooded headlights picked up barbed wire and a gate.

"First Army Group?" asked Patch.

"That's it," said Mullins

"Any idea what the 'man' wants?"

Mullins sniffled. Like so many, with the English climate, he'd caught cold. "I think he just wants to buy you all a drink."

Patch sighed. All the way out to Kent for a drink. And it'd been another one of Captain Travis's long, grueling days.

"You knew he got his second star?"

Patch shook his head. "I knew he was up for it."

"Ike was supposed to come down, but something came up. Old blood-and-guts himself pinned it on this afternoon."

They stopped at the gate.

An armed guard climbed onto the runningboard and flashed a blinding light into the cab of the truck.

Mullins took a folded piece of paper from his shirt pocket and handed it to him.

Ahead, just off to the right, there was a Browning heavy machine-gun emplacement. And beyond, in low-key lighting, a beehive of activity.

At the rear of the truck another guard threw open the canvas and shined his light inside. "I've got a head count of six back here," he called.

The first guard went over to a field phone, cranked it, said something, and listened. Then he came back to Mullins' side of the truck and returned the orders. "All right, you're cleared straight in to HQ. When your business is finished, you're cleared straight out. Don't make any wrong turns."

Major Willis showed them in.

Blackford quickly dispensed with the military formalities. "At your ease, gentlemen. At your ease. Be comfortable." He smiled. "That's an order."

There was a bit of good-natured laughter.

Blackford was sitting on his desk, his shirt collar unbuttoned, his tie loosened.

"Congratulations, sir," said Patch.

They shook hands.

"Thank you, Charles," said Blackford. "Thank you very much."

There were introductions.

Blackford looked each in the eye in turn, and nodded.

Some smiled. Some nodded. The Nazi colonel clicked his heels.

"Thank you for coming," said Blackford.

A smile or two. When a general invites, and sends his

chariot, one attends.

"And you're wondering why." He looked around. They obviously were.

"As some of you know, I've been in on . . . this mission of yours from the beginning. And I wanted to take this last opportunity to wish you the best . . . not luck, though. I know you're the kind of men that will make your own luck."

There was a murmur of appreciation.

He held up his collar. The two stars gleamed. He smiled. "And then there's the matter of a certain recent promotion." He leaned back to a desk drawer. And brought out a large bottle.

"Scotch whiskey, gentlemen. The finest . . . hell, I don't think money can buy it. Takes a general with pull."

Laughter.

"And, truth is, I couldn't think of anyone I'd rather have a drink with."

And they liked that.

"We have some cups around here somewhere," he said to Major Willis.

Willis looked in the metal cabinet, and then went to the broom closet that was just behind and to one side of Blackford.

Blackford opened the bottle of Scotch, sniffed, and nodded his approval.

The broom closet was a small, unlighted affair. Just the light from the main room. Willis would rummage around briefly, and come up with a handful of Dixie cups. And then, as he turned, he would brush the dust cover from the large map that was leaning against the wall in there. He would quickly replace it.

There would just be a moment. And the light would be poor. But trained aerial observers identified enemy aircraft in less.

And anything more wouldn't ring true.

The Calais area of the coast of France. The Straits of Dover. It was the attack map for Operation Fortitude.

Just about *now*.

Blackford watched their eyes.

And then the door to the broom closet closed.

He couldn't be sure. But he thought so. At least some of them. The English captain had turned the other way, but he wasn't going anyway.

Drinks were poured all around.

"There used to be a toast," said Blackford. "Went something like this. 'Here's to it. If you don't get it tonight, may you never get it again.' "

A bit of laughter.

"But then that's not quite appropriate, is it?" He turned serious, and held up his cup. "To you, gentlemen. To your success. May God be with you."

The ride back was a quiet one. The lateness of the hour. The cold of the night. The warmth of the Scotch. And the hum of the heater in the cab. Patch'd dozed for a time.

"Major Patch?" said Mullins, breaking into the stillness.

"Mmm."

"Take me with you."

Patch sat up and looked at Mullins. He knew what he meant. But he wondered how he knew it.

"Bartenders, drivers . . . they just naturally seem to learn things," said Mullins, answering the unasked question.

In the dim light of the cab Patch studied the aging PFC.

"I joined this man's army to fight for my country, sir,"

said Mullins. "And God dammit to hell, that's what I want to do."

"No," said Patch. "I'm sorry."

"Please, sir. It means an awful lot to me."

"I've known people," said Patch, "that would take you along, and then stick a knife in your back just to be cautious."

That observation clearly startled Mullins.

"Forget what you know," said Patch.

16

Captain Travis was standing over him like a hawk. Making sure that none of the pages found their way into his pockets.

It would hardly do for a Nazi soldier to be found with a letter from the USA, now would it?

They were in the stand-by shack. And it was only minutes now until they boarded.

The letter was addressed to him at Fort Bliss, Texas. And in the military way of things it'd somehow caught up with him in amazingly short order.

The familiar writing. He tore it open. And in the distance her perfume. Her. Or was it just him?

My Dearest Andy:

I love you. I know what you're probably thinking. And I don't blame you. You're probably trying to decide whether to even read this letter. Please read, my darling. Oh please read.

I'm not pregnant, Andy. And I didn't marry Homer. I know that doesn't make up for things. My not being pregnant, I mean.

Do you still love me? A little bit? Could you ever find it in your heart to forgive me?

I love you so very much. And I need you. In that

special way.

Honestly, Andy, with Homer it just happened. It never meant anything to me. Really!

I'm sitting here on my bed, upstairs, writing this. And I'm getting goosebumps just thinking about you, and the way you look when you want me.

Andy, if you'll phone, or send a wire, I'll come to you right away. Even if it's the middle of the night. And if you don't want me as your wife, then I'd be proud to live with you as your — whatever they call it. See how worldly I am? I don't even know what they call women like me.

Please want me, Andy. Please take me back. I'll make it up to you. I promise. I'll be so good to you. I'll spend the rest of our lives making you happy.

Waiting,

All my love,
Your Mary Sue

Tears were streaming down his face.

"You all right?" asked Travis.

Holt nodded, wiping his face.

Travis took the letter from him. "I can destroy it, or hold it for you."

Holt tried to smile. "Hold it for me. I'm coming back."

Travis took hold of Holt's shoulder and squeezed briskly. "You're bloody fucking right you are, son."

"Motherfucker!" said the young corporal to the equally young sergeant. "Would you look at that!"

The source of his amazement was the six men sitting in the stand-by shack. Waiting. And the reason for his amazement was their appearance.

113

All wore snow-white jumpsuits. And the uniform insignia that showed at the collar was that of the Nazi Schutzstaffel. The gear piled near the door was equally foreign. Including the six Schmeisser submachine guns.

Two of the men seemed vaguely familiar to the corporal. But he couldn't place them. He followed the sergeant on out into the night to their Flying Fortress. The "Waltzing Mathilda."

"Major Charles Patch?"

"I'm Patch."

"Mercheson," said the first lieutenant. "I'm your pilot."

They shook hands.

"We're running for the ballbearing plant at Steyr, Austria, Major," he said.

They turned and walked slowly toward the other side of the room.

"Maybe seventy, eighty miles from the Berghof."

Patch looked at him.

"I'm not supposed to know what this is all about, Major. But hell, I can read a map as well as the next man."

Patch nodded.

"My orders are verbal. At grid coordinates known only to myself, the 'Waltzing Mathilda' will malfunction both starboard engines. I'll call for, and receive permission for an attempted solo return. I'll pull off a ways, not far, and put you people through the bomb door. Then I'll rejoin my group for the run. Malfunction cleared."

"Sounds good," said Patch.

First Lieutenant Mercheson could no longer contain himself. He grinned. "I'll get you there, Major. Gawddammit, I'll put you within six inches of your drop zone." He shook his head. "Son of a bitch."

114

The four 1,200-horsepower Wright engines popped and banged as the "Waltzing Mathilda" loped along the grass strip. Then she creaked to a stop, and if anything her engines ran rougher. Enough to give a non-'17 crew member serious doubts.

Nearby, in the moonlight, an ambulance watched and waited. A cigarette glowed from the cab. They probably wouldn't be needed now, but they definitely would on the return. And they would be there.

There was a vehicle next to the ambulance. The fire-eaters. They could count on a free drink in any bar they went into, if a '17 crew member was there. For they were the men who went into the flaming, sometimes exploding, mass of tangled steel that was left when a crippled '17 came home. To try and bring out the human destruction.

They frequently gave their lives. And many had been horribly maimed.

Most '17 crew members agreed, they'd rather risk another run than trade.

On the wooden catwalk outside the control tower a man raised his arm. A flare arched toward the stars.

The "Mathilda" turned into the wind, and went to full throttles. The engines cleared, and 55,000 pounds of medium bomber began bouncing across what had probably been a cow pasture just a few years previous.

Off to one side, an ack-ack crew in full battle gear manned their gun, probably glad to be where they were, for the moment at least. They waved.

The "Mathilda" gathered steam and tried to fly. But Mercheson held her down.

Finally, as the trees at the end of the strip raced for them, she lifted off. The gear came clanking up.

Just a few hundred feet off the English countryside, the engines throttled back and the "Mathilda" began to hedge-hop. Irritate the locals? Hell, they love it. It meant their skies were theirs. And Jerry was going to get some more of his.

As they neared the Channel they began to climb. They went to oxygen masks and headsets. The temperature began to drop.

"All right," came the order, "make sure those Gawd-damned things work."

Bolts were worked. And twelve .50 caliber machine guns "cleared their throats" with short bursts. Empty brass clanked. Tracers arched out into the moonlight.

To the left, the right, above, below, behind, other '17s began forming on them. A vast armada. To deal pain, death, and destruction. And to receive it. Not all would come home.

The corporal at the waist gun kept glancing at the "Mathilda's" passengers every so often. Especially Hastings and Joubert. Obviously trying to jog his memory as to just where he'd seen them before.

Hastings and Joubert were amused. Should they tell him? Or let him chew on it?

Suddenly, fingers of light began probing the sky around them. And as quickly, there were explosions.

Flak," screamed someone, identifying the obvious.

A round exploded just below them. The "Mathilda" lurched and yawed in the shock waves.

To their left a sister ship took a near direct hit, losing most of one wing. She immediately flew into the nonexistent wing and then began a crazy, flopping spin downwards. There were no parachutes.

"Close up, close up," screamed someone in command.

Another Fortress moved into the place of the fallen '17.

Abruptly the flak ceased. The searchlights went out.

Nothing but the quiet, comfortable roar of the four engines. The moonlit sky. An occasional bluish cloud slipping past.

A head count was taken.

Only the one.

A feeling of relief, that it was someone else. And a feeling of guilt for that thought. But there were the odds. Always the odds.

Only the one.

17

The moon was gone. To the east the sky was turning gray. The dawn was coming. It would be soon now.

Tension was mounting. Both the crew of the "Waltzing Mathilda" and the six in white jumpsuits. First-timers. Oldtimers. No matter that you've tasted battle. The wait before the tempest is the worst thing about it all. The man who says otherwise has either never experienced it, or he is a liar.

Each man handles it in his own way. Some talk incessantly. Some are very quiet. Some even sleep. But inside, all are crying.

"Bandits! Bandits!"

"Where, Gawddammit?"

The reply was a soft, slow Louisiana drawl. "Shit, Lieutenant, all over the fuckin' sky."

The gunners went to work. Cool Methodical. Each had a piece of the Fortress to defend. And if each did his job . . .

There was a heavy pounding. A German fighter shot past. Very, very close. As though the "Mathilda" were standing still. Hundreds, maybe thousands, of tracers followed. The fighter exploded. Where there'd once been a man and a plane, there was nothing. Just a puff of smoke.

There were cheers. "We're hit! We're hit!"

The '17 just to the right and above was streaming smoke. Then flames began licking across her fuselage.

Another voice. "Captain's dead! Jump! Get out, get out!"

And all over the sky, perhaps even in the enemy planes, those who could were watching and counting.

One. Two Three. And three 'chutes opened.

Map positions were noted.

There was a long wait.

Then three more. But they were on fire. Their parachutes. Their clothing. Their bodies. And they were still alive. You could tell.

They were the last.

"Hail Mary, full of grace, blessed art thou . . . " The voice trailed off.

The burning '17 flew with them for what seemed like a long time. Then she slid into a turning dive, as though returning home.

The German fighters broke off at the same time. Probably fuel and ammunition for just a short sortie.

The corporal turned from his waist-gun and moved unsteadily over to Joubert. He sat down on the Frenchman's lap. His eyes were clouded. And there was a gaping, bloody wound in the upper chest.

Joubert clamped his hand across the wound.

"Momma? Daddy?"

"Yes," said Joubert. "Yes." He put his arm around the corporal and held him. Patting. Soothing. Rocking him on his knee.

Some watched. Some turned away.

"I'm going to die," said the corporal.

And he did.

The malfunction, when it came, seemed in earnest, particularly in the aftermath of the German fighter attack. The "Waltzing Mathilda" veered sharply, trying to fly into its ailing starboard engines. A situation that can quickly become dangerous.

Skill in the cockpit controlled, and the '17 resumed course. Airspeed dropped. They began falling behind.

There was a flurry of slang radio traffic.

The "Mathilda" began a long sweeping turn to the right.

And then they were alone. A most naked feeling indeed.

The bomb-bay doors cranked open. The icy roaring wind tore at them. The very big, frightening step into the unknown awaited.

And it was the time when most men have to fight themselves to keep from backing out, from turning and running away.

They were joined by First Lieutenant Mercheson, glancing repeatedly at his watch. He seemed to be searching for something to say. That right something or another. He didn't find it. He spoke only to Hastings. "Give 'em hell, Tommy," he said.

Hastings smiled. "I'll do it, mate."

Another glance at the watch. "Now."

Patch took a deep breath, and jumped.

The others followed.

Holt was last. He hesitated, and then jumped.

Mercheson watched them disappear.

And then a seventh man was beside him. Like the others he wore a snow-white jumpsuit.

"Hurry," said Mercheson.

The man nodded.

And he was gone.

Sirens screeched. Beneath the camouflage netting the generators were chugging. The smokescreen was forming.

In the Berghof people in various states of dress and undress were descending the sixty-five steps to the bunker. Yawning. Sleep-filled faces. Hair askew.

The air raids had become so frequent that many had taken to ignoring them. And the Führer had delivered a stern luncheon lecture on such stupidity.

Now the Führer stood at the entrance, anxiously scanning the skies. He was fully dressed. He probably had not yet been to bed.

Since Willi obviously could not go to a place of safety ahead of the Führer, he took up a position nearby, and waited.

Hitler nodded pleasantly, and resumed his watch. After a while he turned to Willi, a hint of amusement in his eyes. "Do you suppose there could be any heavy sleepers who haven't heard the alarm?"

"I'll make certain, *mein Führer.*"

Willi quickly checked the bedrooms, feeling a bit like an intruder, though not really expecting to find anyone either. And he didn't.

On his return he noticed a light showing beneath the door to one of the pantries. On impulse he pushed the door open. And quickly wished he hadn't.

Martin Bormann was in the process of seducing a young woman.

Her blouse was open, her breasts exposed. Small breasts. The breasts of a young girl.

It was Heidi. One of the girls from the kitchen. No more than fifteen or sixteen. With her sandy hair and rosy cheeks she looked quite a lot like Willi's little sister.

Her bloomers were on the floor. Her skirt was up

around her waist. Bormann had her pinned back against a butcher block, forcing her legs apart.

She was fighting. But not too much. There were tears and terror in her eyes. She was mouthing the word "no." Over and over and over.

A strange scene. A totally silent rape.

Both Bormann and Heidi looked at Willi.

"Well?"

"The air raid . . . " stammered Willi.

"So go to the shelter."

"But . . . "

"Please make him stop . . . " A bare whisper. Her legs were apart now.

Bormann unbuttoned his pants. An icy look at Willi. Then he reached into his pants.

Willi hurried from the pantry.

A long low moan. Then a soft sobbing.

Willi cursed himself. Hated himself. He was a coward. He vowed to seek reassignment. This very instant.

But no. There was Hannah.

Hannah sat up in bed. The sirens. Again.

She lay back, and pulled the covers over her head.

Maybe one day the bombs would rain on the Berghof. And it would all be over.

She peeked out. It was quiet.

She pulled the covers back over her head, remembering when she'd been a little girl and that'd made everything safe. But no longer.

She hopped out of bed, and slipped out of her floor-length flannel gown. Her nipples quickly erected in the cold.

She went over to the dresser. A huge, beautiful old piece that'd been in the family almost a hundred years.

122

But the mirror was wavy.

She stepped close. There were little wrinkles around her eyes. She was getting old. She smoothed the skin around her eyes. No she wasn't. She was hardly older than Willi. And he hadn't said anything.

She cupped her breasts in her hands. They were full. But they didn't sag. Not really.

She turned and took a couple of steps away from the dresser, looking over her shoulder. Willi thought that was nice. And she guessed he was right.

She went back to the dresser, and again smoothed the skin around her eyes. It was probably just from sleep. Or the lack of it. She hadn't been sleeping well lately.

What if Willi were to walk in right now? She giggled out loud. She knew perfectly well what would happen.

Then she remembered. She hurriedly dressed.

The sirens again. But this time it was the all-clear.

18

Patch pulled the ripcord. The 'chute streamed out, and then billowed open with a comfortable jerk.

There was a lazy, floating sensation. But it was deceiving. It'd been a high-altitude low-open jump. The snowy alpine meadow was coming up fast. And there were gusting surface winds.

Patch slipped the 'chute, hit, rolled, and was back on his feet collapsing the 'chute. A near textbook perfect landing.

The others were working their 'chutes, coming down nearby.

Except for the one. He was going into the trees. He was fighting his 'chute, literally trying to run across the sky away from the timber, his legs absolutely churning.

Patch started to yell, but in this kind of country sound could carry for miles. His 'chute removed now, the almost automatic body count hit him. Seven! He made for the trees as fast as the snow would allow.

The man struck the peak of a huge Bavarian Pine. And for a time it looked as though he was going to make it, the tearing 'chute breaking his fall just enough.

But then, some twenty feet or so from the ground, his leg caught in the veenotch of a limb. An audible crack. And a horrible scream.

Even from where he stood, Patch could see the bloody thighbone protruding through the white jumpsuit.

Mercifully, Mullins had passed out.

He'd just rested his saw against the stack of wood for a breather, and lighted his pipe, when the scream echoed through the woods.

He'd jumped, and almost dropped his pipe. It was that close.

Just a few steps. And he could see them. People in these parts were a rarity. He should know. He'd been cutting the downed timber around here for more than thirty years.

Two of them climbed a tree.

The woodcutter quickly understood their predicament, and started forth to lend a hand.

One of them, on the ground, was burying their parachutes.

Strange.

The two in the tree gently freed their injured comrade. Then one of them called down to the others.

The woodcutter stopped. And then quickly stepped behind a tree. It was a language he'd never heard before. He peeked out.

They were lowering the man by his parachute lines.

Their markings were SS. The woodcutter'd seen enough of them in Berchtesgaden to know that. Maybe they were Poles or Finns. Volunteers for money. He'd heard there were such. But somehow he didn't think so.

They cut off the man's pant's leg, and sprinkled something on his injury. A terrible injury. They gave him an injection. And then began wrapping him up.

That's the thing. Keep him good and warm. The woodcutter looked around. He was at that age where caution and curiosity are constantly at odds with each other.

Caution took the upper hand. He would head deeper into the woods. Just in case they discovered he'd been there. Then he'd angle back for his cart, and make for Berchtesgaden.

It was probably nothing, but he'd report it anyway. They'd give him a big glass of schnapps. No matter. He'd heard that Spaatz fellow was good about that sort of thing.

He turned, and moved out at a shuffle. Something he could keep up all day long. The envy of many a man half his age.

They'd turned the remaining 'chute into a litter for Mullins and were about to get under way, when Patch and Joubert picked up on it. They looked at each other.

Tobacco. Pipe tobacco.

By then the others had noticed it too.

Silently, quickly, they spread out, machine pistols at the ready, seeking the source.

Hastings pointed.

Like well-trained infantry taking a machine gun nest, they moved forward. Tree by tree. One or two at a time. And always, someone just behind SS Colonel Max Wolff. Empty magazines or not.

Holt stepped around a tree, expecting the unexpected. That was where he'd been. But he was gone. With a hand signal he brought the others in.

The spoor said it all. The saw against the pile of wood. The tracks starting forward. Stopping. Going behind the tree. Fidgeting. Then moving off in a hurry.

A woodcutter had seen them. Heard them speak English. And was going to report them.

Patch took a deep breath, and let it out. Shit. He

126

should've put a couple of men out on perimeter. The Mullins thing had taken them all by surprise. But dammit, that was what he was paid for.

He looked at the little group. It would take two on the litter. And in the heavy snow, two to relieve. And someone had to be on top of the good colonel at all times. If and when he decided to bolt.

And by the book, he should stay with the main group. Fuck the book. But this time the book was probably right.

He pointed to Hastings and Joubert. "Get him."

They nodded, the challenge of the hunt in their eyes.

"We're dead if you don't," said Patch. "And remember. It's his backyard."

They stopped for a moment.

The trick is to hurry, but not too much. Take time to read the sign. Otherwise you may overrun your quarry. Or worse. Walk into his trap. Hunting a man who thinks you might be after him isn't as easy as most people think.

"The bloody bastard hasn't stopped yet," said Hastings softly.

Joubert put his hands on his hips and looked around their little piece of the wilderness. Nothing but snow and huge trees. Silent but for their heavy breathing. And the occasional chunk of snow breaking loose from a branch. Startling them each and every time. "Has my sense of direction failed me altogether?"

At first Hastings wondered what the Frenchman had seen that he hadn't. Then it began to dawn on him, too. "And remember. It's his backyard." That was what the Yank had said. He took out compass and map, found the meadow where they'd landed, and traced his finger at the approximate angle. "I'll be a son of a bitch."

"The goose chase," said Joubert.

They'd been fairly close to the only road around when they'd landed. And they'd been angling steadily away from it ever since.

"He intends simply to outrun us," said Joubert. "Wear us down. Then cut back to the road."

Hastings put the map away. "And if he gets there before we do . . . "

Joubert nodded, drawing a finger across his throat.

Hastings moved out, leaving the woodcutter's trail. Compass in hand. Making straight for the road. He broke into a near trot. A killing pace, considering.

The Frenchman was hard on his heels.

Patch and Weinberg eased the litter down as gently as they could. Both were gasping for breath.

Mullins moaned.

Wolff knelt beside the injured man. The muzzle of the silenced Walther P-38 in Holt's hand never left him. "You still don't trust me," he said, matter-of-factly.

"No," said Patch.

"Then why ask me along?"

"Frankly, back at Bliss — on paper — it seemed a hell of a lot better idea than it does right now."

Wolff nodded, understanding. He loosened the dressing and sprinkled more sulfa.

"How is he?" asked Weinberg.

"Don't be absurd," said Wolff briskly. He looked at the OSS captain. "The infection has already begun. The shock has had its effect." He motioned with his hand. "The temperature. Soon, gangrene."

"Will you?" asked Patch.

"Will I?"

"We've seen your file," said Weinberg.

Wolff smiled thinly. "I'm flattered that you think I

could. But it's been years. And I never completed my medical training."

Mullins moaned. His eyes blinked open. Wild at first. Then calmer as he focused on Patch. A friendly face.

"God, it hurts," he said.

Patch nodded.

"How bad am I?"

Patch hesitated.

"It's quite possible you will die," said Wolff, "unless you receive proper medical attention very, very soon."

Mullins had little color, but he paled even more.

"Wolff, God dammit," said Patch.

"Herr Mullins is not a child," said Wolff. "He deserves to be told the truth. To make his own peace with his own God. While he is still able."

Mullins was obviously frightened, but he seemed to accept the pronouncement, too.

Wolff stroked his cheek. "When the pain becomes too much again, tell me. We have morphine."

For a long moment, the little group was silent.

"Let's move out," said Patch.

19

The woodcutter stepped gingerly out of the woods onto the road near the horse and cart. He looked around cautiously.

Quickly he picked up the weight, climbed up onto the cart, and gave the horse a coaxing tap on the rump with the reins.

The ancient animal began her usual plodding walk.

He still had the feeling he wasn't alone. But then he wasn't. Back there somewhere there were some soldiers.

He smiled. If they were following him, they were back there by quite a few meters. Searching for their breath.

He felt better. To tell the truth, he'd been more than a little frightened.

Maybe they were Hungarians. No, somehow . . .

He'd just started around a slight bend in the road when the two soldiers came into view.

He drew in his breath. But they weren't wearing the white parachute clothing.

They smiled and waved. The one was a giant of a man. The other a bit of a dumpling.

He waved back. Two of the Fatherland's finest. They'd see to things.

But then what were two soldiers doing up here, just walking around? And the dumpling didn't even look German.

He popped the reins across Bertha's back, hard. The startled old mare leaped forward, spilling much of the wood from the cart.

The soldiers were drawing their handguns now.

Bertha broke into a full gallop. Something she hadn't done in over sixteen years for certain. The cart slithered on the ice and snow.

As he drew near, the woodcutter began throwing wood. Much of it missed, but it distracted them. And then he had some luck. A piece struck the big fellow in the shoulder, and glanced into the face of the dumpling.

And then he was past them. He hunkered down. And concentrated on staying aboard.

The blow had knocked the pistol from Hastings's hand. He took Joubert's. The Frenchman was temporarily out of it anyway, holding his bleeding face.

The Englishman forced himself to take his time. Then he began stroking the trigger. There was little more than the sound of the slide and the ejecting brass.

But nothing. And the Walther was empty.

Bloody German gun. With the Browning he'd have put fourteen in the boiler room.

Then the woodcutter clutched his shoulder. He was hit. But it wasn't enough.

Hastings considered the Schmeisser. But it wasn't silenced. And the range was quickly becoming too much for it, too.

He scooped up the other P-38 and started down the road at a run.

"For God's sakes, *mon ami*, you can't outrun a horse."

But the Englishman meant to try.

And Joubert came chugging after him.

Bertha slowed. The woodcutter let her. She deserved it.

And they should be nearly out of harm's way by now.

He wondered whether he should stop at Fräulein Müller's, and take her to safety with him. Her place was just around the next bend. Maybe her lover, the young soldier, would be there. He'd know what to do. But if he wasn't . . .

He wondered how badly he was injured. There was quite a bit of blood. But it didn't hurt too much. He didn't know about such things. Maybe he was dying.

Bertha slowed even more, and then stopped altogether. She began to tremble. At first in different places. And then all over, violently.

The woodcutter climbed down.

As he did so, the horse collapsed.

"Oh, no." He got down beside her.

She was dead.

Slowly he got back to his feet. There were tears in his eyes. He looked back up the empty road they'd just descended. He shook his fist. "You'll pay," he said quietly. "Damn you forever to hell, you'll pay."

Is no one home? The woodcutter pounded again, shaking the door on its hinges. "Fräulein Müller? Let me in! Hurry!" He glanced back toward the road.

Finally the curtain parted. Fräulein Müller peeked out. Then the door opened. But just a bit.

"Yes? What . . . You're hurt."

"The enemy," he said. "The British I think. Maybe the Americans. Is your soldier friend here?"

"No he . . ."

"Then do you have a gun?"

"No . . ."

"A shotgun perhaps . . . " He pushed past her. And he saw the reason for her reluctance.

The door closed.

Four of them. Plus the injured man. In the uniform of the Schutzstaffel.

"Do not be afraid, old one," said the one with the scar across his face. "I will see to your wound. No further harm will come to you."

The woodcutter stared at him. He was German. He had to be.

He turned to Hannah. It was the most puzzling thing of his life.

But she looked away.

Hannah Müller's door opened.

Hastings came out of the woods at a slogging run. A Walther P-38 in each hand. One empty. One loaded. Sweat was streaming down his face.

Inside, he wobbled, glanced at the woodcutter, and then bent over, sucking in air in huge gasps. He was nearly out of it.

Moments later Joubert made his appearance. Staggering. But still moving at something resembling a run. The bleeding from the nose had dwindled to a trickle, but it felt like a balloon. Some ways back he'd begun throwing up. Now he had the dry heaves.

Inside, he quickly moved away from the others. His dry heaving continued.

Hastings pointed up with the empty Walther. "Scout plane."

And then they all heard it.

It buzzed low overhead. Circled. And then went on. They waited. But it didn't return.

"Did they see you?" asked Patch.

Hastings shook his head. " . . . don't think so . . . into the woods . . . "

"Perhaps you would wish me to just amputate," said Wolff, the dark humor showing in his eyes.

Joubert was sullen, not answering, not taking the bait.

Patch hovered nearby.

"It would be a distinct cosmetic improvement," continued Wolff.

Still no answer.

Wolff smoothed the tape gently around Joubert's nose. "It is soundly broken, but it will mend. You will live. Nothing less than a bullet for you. Right there." He tapped him once between the eyes, and removed his hand just as the Frenchman took a swipe at it.

He crossed the loft.

The woodcutter started to smile, but then checked it. He had not yet decided if Wolff was a traitor in fact or somehow a friend in disguise.

Now that was a lucky wound. The kind that many on the Eastern Front prayed for. Probably enough to get you home for a while. And still whole.

Patch and Mullins were talking.

And the comfortable feeling of having seen to the pain of others left him.

Mullins stopped talking as he joined them, but then, with a gesture that said it made no difference, he continued. "Anyway, when you work for a general you get to know the ins and outs. It was easy to put together some forged papers." He smiled. "That pilot thought I was on some kind of secret mission for Ike himself."

Patch sighed and shook his head.

Wolff put his hand on Mullins's forehead, and then felt his pulse. "The pain?"

"Better again. But that stuff you gave me doesn't seem to be helping as much."

Patch took Wolff by the arm. Together they took a

short walk across the hayloft.

Patch looked at him.

"Bad," said Wolff.

"Then I want you to operate."

"I told you . . . That isn't just a broken leg."

"I know what you told me. There isn't any other choice."

"I could very well cripple him. Or worse."

"There isn't any other choice."

Wolff nodded. He'd about reached the same decision himself. Books and procedures of years ago. It frightened him. More than any combat he'd ever experienced.

20

"The aeroplane reported what?" Spaatz looked up from the file.

"A dead horse, sir," said Meyer. "Still harnessed to a two-wheeled cart."

Spaatz looked at him.

"Approximately there, sir," said Meyer, pointing on the plastic covered map that made up the top of Spaatz's desk.

"And?"

"And?"

"What else?"

"That's it, sir."

A moment's silence.

"I fail to understand the military significance," said Spaatz. "Is it blocking the road?"

"Not that I know of, sir."

"Does it represent some threat to the Führer that I am unable to comprehend?"

Meyer shook his head. But he stood his ground. If he failed to report it, and Spaatz found out he hadn't reported it . . . And for that exact reason the pilot had reported it to him.

"Then what? Please."

"Your standing orders, Hauptsturmführer, are to

report everything," said Meyer. "Everything."

Spaatz nodded. "That is correct, Herr Meyer. And you may consider it reported. Thank you." He picked up the file.

"Shall I send a couple of men to look into it, sir?"

He put the file down again. "How many horses?"

"One, sir."

"Then send one man. When someone is finished with their regular duties. I do not see an urgency."

"*Jawohl*." Meyer clicked his heels.

Technically, the operation had been a success. They'd just brought Mullins back up to the hay loft. And none too soon. Hannah Müller's young SS friend had arrived moments later.

They'd used the kitchen table for the surgery. Plenty of light. Close to the stove for warmth and the sterilizing. And the medical bag that Captain Travis had sent along had been surprisingly complete.

Mullins moaned.

Wolff stroked his cheek gently, and looked around.

Patch and Weinberg were on the watch. The rest were sleeping, or seemed to be.

They weren't keeping too close an eye on him anymore. An opportunity would be coming.

And then what? Turn them in? Unlikely as it seemed, what if they did manage to get to Hitler? A quick peace in the West, and the might of the Wehrmacht turned to the East. Much of Germany might yet be saved.

And if he didn't turn them in, then what? As the Major had put it, it'd all seemed a better idea back at Fort Bliss, Texas.

Mullins moaned again.

Wolff bent close to his chest and listened. Pneumonia

was the danger now.

Bubbles?

He wasn't sure. His ears were no longer what they used to be.

Too many explosives.

Willi sat up. "What's that?"

"What?"

"Listen."

"What?"

"It sounds like someone is moaning."

Hannah listened. "It's the wind, Dummkopf." She pushed him back down. "This is a very old house."

"Oh." He squeezed her on the behind, and put the pillow back over his head.

Soon he was asleep again. She could tell.

They'd better keep the man quiet. Thankfully, there was some wind. And it helped.

A tear made its way across her cheek. Then another. She let go, sobbing softly into her pillow.

Willi'd asked her what was wrong when they were making love. Just some cramps, she'd said. Her monthly was coming due.

How'd it all ever come about?

How, indeed.

Hannah'd just turned sixteen that spring. A bitter young girl. One of the few not caught up in the enthusiasm of the times.

It was a beautiful spring though. Everything in bloom.

It'd been a Sunday. And she'd gone to the park. Just to enjoy the freshness of everything. She'd stopped to watch some children at play, kicking a ball.

She'd noticed him right away of course. But she'd

pretended not to. So young and handsome. Dashing — that was the one word that fit him the best. The thin mustache that was popular in those times. And the dancing eyes.

He'd walked over to her. "Hello."

She'd smiled, and turned back to watch the children. "It would be nice if we could join them, wouldn't it?" She'd smiled again.

He had an easy way about him. And she soon found herself drawn into conversation with him. They talked of everything and nothing. The weather. The flowers.

He was quite a bit older than her. At least it seemed so then. She'd never known for sure. Maybe twenty or twenty-two. Swiss. Or so he'd said.

Johann Koch. He had an apartment near the park. And though he lived in Munich he traveled throughout Europe. An independent salesman of Walther firearms.

They walked. He bought frozen desserts for them from a stand.

He showed her his car. A dark blue Mercedes roadster. Not a new one. But a Mercedes nevertheless.

The next evening he took her to dinner. And then he took her to bed. Her first love.

Spring turned to summner. And Hannah and Johann were inseparable. She moved into his apartment. She'd hated hers anyway. But there'd been nowhere else, and no one else. Just an elderly aunt. And she was in a rest-home.

She traveled with him. To the Walther factory at Zella-Mehlis. To Poland and Czechoslovakia. And back to Munich. Then north to Holland. And a swing south through Belgium, France, and Switzerland. Along the German border.

They stayed at picturesque little roadside inns. And frequently retired at such an early hour that it was em-

139

barrassing to look the innkeeper in the eye the next morning.

But Johann was insatiable. And so was she.

It was in early September that they began to suspect that they were being followed.

At first Johann just laughed it off. But Hannah could tell that it bothered him.

Then he decided to put it to the test. He took a corner at speed, and then quickly braked so that they were moving quite slow.

Sure enough, the black sedan that'd been pacing them came roaring up on their tail. It hesitated, apparently unsure what to do, and then backed off.

But why?

Hannah decided it must be because of the expensive engraved Walther pistols Johann kept in the trunk of the Mercedes as samples.

But someone would be foolish to try and rob them. Johann always kept a loaded Walther PP of his own nearby.

21

It was late when they stopped. Just inside Germany. They went straight to their room.

Hannah quickly undressed and got into bed. It'd been two days. Because of that damned black automobile. But they hadn't seen it now since early morning.

Tomorrow they would be back in Munich. A week or two of nothing but love. Sleeping late. Reading the newspapers.

And tonight there would be love. Hannah couldn't believe how anxious she was. In such a short time.

Johann blew out the candle, and undressed. He was still shy that way.

Hannah smiled to herself in the dark. That was the only way he was shy.

He came to the bed.

She reached for him. And found him.

Then he moved away. To look out the window one more time.

He cursed. And began fumbling back into his clothes. "Quickly," he hissed.

She hurried from the bed, and started to light the candle.

"*Nein!*" Then more softly. "We'll just slip away."

"We could inform the police, now that . . . "

He looked at her.

There was just enough moonlight in the room to make out his features. She would remember that look. And, vaguely, she was beginning to understand.

There was a backstairs, and they took it.

The driver of the black sedan was no longer making any attempt to be subtle. He'd parked next to their Mercedes.

They watched the car for a minute or two. But no one was in it.

Quickly across the courtyard now. Each sound louder than it really was. Suspicious of every shadow. Like two thieves in the night.

Johann helped Hannah into the passenger side of the roadster, putting the only bag they'd taken in on her lap. He left the door ajar and started around the car.

And absolutely out of nowhere a man appeared. Dressed mostly in black. A pistol in his hand.

Johann froze.

Hannah nearly jumped out of her skin.

"You are under arrest, Herr Koch." Not at all the menacing voice that was expected.

Arrest? Hannah mouthed the words.

". . . or whatever your name might be.   I charge you with being a spy."

A spy?

The man took out handcuffs.

And that seemed to frighten Johann. More than the gun.

Their eyes met. Those dancing eyes. And they were speaking to Hannah.

Until now the man had not paid too much attention to Hannah. Her age and her sex undoubtedly. But he caught the look. "You will please to step out of the car,

Fräulein," he said, almost kindly. "And you will please to stay so that I can see you."

Hannah nodded dumbly. She put the bag over onto the driver's seat. And as she did so her hand found the Walther PP 7.65 mm that was snugged between the seats.

It is without question the finest handgun in the world.

She fought her panic, and tried to remember the few times they'd stopped in some woods and fired the gun.

First, disengage the safety.

She moved the lever up with her finger. It clicked.

But the man seemed not to notice.

With the gun at her side, in the folds of her clothing, Hannah got out of the car.

Simply point the gun and pull the trigger. It is double action. The first pull will be rather hard. Thereafter it will be quite soft.

The man glanced at Hannah. Johann's hands were behind his back, the handcuffs in place.

Hannah put the gun out in front of her, and began squeezing the trigger.

The man saw what she was doing. His mouth opened.

And for the next several moments it was like the cinema, where the machine isn't working right, and the pictures moves slowly.

The man's mouth opened more. Time for that. But not time to turn his gun on Hannah.

The Walther exploded. Then again. And again.

The man dropped his gun, and clutched at himself. He went to his knees.

Johann turned and kicked the man in the face, putting him all the way down.

Hannah was shaking her head. She felt the scream coming. But strangely it died in her throat.

Somewhere a dog began barking.

And on the third floor of the inn a light came on. "*Was ist das?*" someone called.

They hunkered down between the cars, next to the dying man.

Shaking, sobbing, Hannah searched the man, looking for the key to the handcuffs. "I'm sorry," she said over and over.

The man nodded weakly.

Did he actually forgive her?

He gasped deeply. Rattled. And he was gone.

The dog stopped barking. The light went out.

And Hannah found the key in the man's shoe. But it was several minutes before she could control her hands enough to take off the handcuffs.

Together they put the body into the back seat of the black sedan.

"Follow me," said Johann hoarsely, getting into the front seat.

A nightmare.

And it would be just that for years to come.

They buried the body in some woods about an hour later. And then abandoned the black sedan in the parking area of the first railroad station they came to.

They drove the remainder of the night, arriving back in Munich just after dawn. They didn't return to their old apartment however, but instead took another a considerable distance away.

They didn't talk about what'd happened, though Hannah wanted to. Johann had withdrawn into himself, and was not unlike a caged animal. He went out frequently. At odd hours.

They made love. But it was no longer the same. Something, that important something, was held back.

Then one morning she awoke to find him gone. No

note. Nothing. She waited. And waited.

Finally, frightened, she left the apartment. Never to return.

She spent the first part of the winter washing dishes in a restaurant near the old neighborhood. Hot and steamy work. But quite welcome, considering the cold water room she lived in.

Then, in the dead of winter, her aunt passed away, leaving her the small, run-down farm near Berchtesgaden. Berchtesgaden.

And Hannah ran to it gladly.

For a long time she lived in fear. Wary of strangers and the occasional knock at the door. Certain that it meant questions about a certain man a certain night. Jumping at the window rattling in the wind.

And the nights. The dream. "I'm sorry, I'm sorry," she'd be saying, over and over. And the man would be nodding. And then the death rattle. She'd wake up in a cold sweat, moaning.

And too, she thought often of Johann. She would hear from him sometime. A letter. Something. Or was he dead? Had he somehow gone to his death protecting her? Her name sealed on his lips? Or had he just run away?

The years rolled by. And the fears, the thoughts of Johann, slipped into the background.

And then, in August of 1939, it all came back to haunt her.

22

Less than a month until the war.

It was hot that August. Like it seldom is in the mountains. Dry. Dusty.

Hannah was outside. Nothing to do for a little bit. Rather enjoying the warmth.

She caught sight of the man. Probably before he caught sight of her. She didn't go inside, but she did look him over closely. Habit.

He was short, and completely bald. Thick glasses. Hiking trousers. A knapsack on his back.

A nature lover on an outing. Probably seeking directions, or maybe a cool drink at the well. Harmless.

She couldn't have been more wrong.

He smiled pleasantly. "Would I be permitted?" He pointed to the well.

She nodded.

"A beautiful day." He ran the bucket down, and back up. He drank from the dipper, and sprinkled the rest on his head. Then he turned and looked at Hannah. Still smiling. "Johnny Cook sends his love."

She stared at the man, not understanding.

"I should say Johann Koch, shouldn't I?"

A bit of a gasp. Her hand started toward her mouth. She recovered quickly. But she'd betrayed herself. So easily.

"He said to tell you he's sorry he had to leave the way he did. But he had his orders. And it was for your safety, too."

Not from the German police . . . ?

"You see, as far as we can tell, they still don't know about you. Yet."

Yet? It was the only threat the British Secret Intelligence Service ever made. But it was enough.

The man took off the knapsack. "I have something for you, Hannah Müller. We'll go inside, and I'll show you how to operate it. Once a week, very precisely, you'll turn it on and listen. But just for a few moments. And every once in a while — not too often — we'll expect a reply."

For the first couple of weeks she left the wireless set hidden in the hayloft. Afraid to be near it. Afraid to get rid of it.

Once, she took it deep into the woods and dug a hole. Then she just looked at the hole, remembering the man she'd killed, and the hole they'd buried him in.

Then in September the war with Poland began. And she began listening.

The man had spoken the truth. They only asked her to answer every few months. Little things. Seemingly unimportant. To be sure she was listening, it seemed, and that she would reply. To draw her tighter into their web.

Their spy in Berchtesgaden.

Once again the passage of time brought with it a sense of security. The war began to go badly. And on the far horizon there was a trace of hope.

She met Willi. "A scavenger for the mess," he'd laughingly called himself. And they'd fallen in love. Real love. He was more man in more ways than Johann could ever hope to be.

He wanted to be her husband, and a woodcutter. Little Hannah. And little Willi.

God, how she loved him.

And God, how she cursed that spring day of her youth when she'd gone to that park in Munich.

Hannah turned on the wireless, allowing a moment or so for it to warm up. Anxious for it to be over with for another week. It still frightened her.

The tail end of a message.

She glanced at her watch, and reached to turn the set off.

Then the message was coming through for her.

She fumbled with pencil and paper, and began taking it down. Then the message was repeated.

She took out the little book, and deciphered. And she was stunned.

Below, her udder swollen with milk, the cow bawled.

"Acknowledge," came the order again.

She acknowledged. And turned the set off.

Prepare yourself. Johann and friends are coming.

But Johann didn't come.

And the ones who did had never heard of him.

Hannah wiped her eyes on the pillowcase.

Somehow . . . some way . . . she and Willi would have a life together. She reached for him. Found him. And began stroking him.

He murmured contentedly. Then he came awake. In more ways than one.

Hannah smiled. "*Ah, mein Willi.*" And she mounted him.

Thad:

I'll just blurt it out. This is a Dear-John letter. There.
I know you never thought you'd be receiving one. And
I never thought I'd be writing one.

I know this is a hell of a way to do things. But frankly,
I just don't have the guts to do it to your face.

I won't do anything until you get home. And then we'll
do whatever needs to be done quietly. I don't want to do
anything to hurt your career. I certainly owe you that.

I know you're asking yourself if there's someone else.
You know very well there've been several. You've just
never wanted to believe it of me. That's the way I am. I'm
sorry.

But no, I'm not leaving you for anyone else. Just for
me. No longer the actor on the military stage.

I'm going to take what's left of my life, and just be me.

You know, Thad, I feel better already.

I'm sorry,
Adele

Very slowly, Blackford crumpled the letter into a tight
little ball. Then, as slowly, he smoothed it out again.

Several.

His jaw muscle worked. The surest way to shatter a
man's ego. Destroy him. But he'd be damned.

He had wondered at times. But then why should she?
He'd climbed higher . . . further . . . And he'd satisfied
her in bed, too. He was sure of that.

Or had he?

Several.

Who? One always wonders who. Somehow it's important. To compare.

A shavetail? A company sergeant? No. Not Adele.

A major, perhaps. Yes, for one, a major.

And he'd known all the time.

"Pneumonia," said Wolff.

"Are you sure?" asked Patch.

"Yes."

Patch and Weinberg looked at the German colonel.

Wolff threw up his hands in a gesture of despair. "What can I tell you? He should be in a hospital. And even that . . . "

Patch nodded. His mood was black. A badly injured man. A prisoner. And the clock was running against them. What else . . .

A motorcycle?

SS-Mann Kruger dismounted from the motorcycle, and put the kick stand down.

The kick stand buried itself, and the motorcycle tipped over.

He cursed and kicked the machine. It'd gone out from under him twice on the way up. He wiped some of the slush from his uniform, and pushed the goggles up over his eyes.

Just to investigate a damned dead horse. He walked over to the carcass, and threw his arm up in a stiff Nazi salute.

Jawohl, Herr Spaatz. I have investigated the matter of the horse. And, after much deliberation, I have concluded that it is indeed a horse, and it is dead. And I have also looked into the matter of the cart. And — would you believe it — it is a cart.

And furthermore . . . Just a minute. What's this?

Blood. There by the horse. On the seat of the cart. And leading off that way.

Someone had been rather severely injured, and had run their horse to death seeking aid.

He couldn't begin to guess how it could be of concern to the SS. But then he wasn't going to go back and put the question to Hauptsturmführer Spaatz either.

150

Kruger set off following the tracks.

23

"Blow the mission?" Major Willis made no attempt to hide his amazement at what he'd just heard

"That's the necessary conclusion," said Blackford. "Now listen to the reasoning."

Willis waited.

"You've felt from the start that they have no chance whatsoever of succeeding. And I agree."

"That's right, sir. But . . . "

"In a matter of weeks, maybe less, the largest invasion force ever assembled on the face of the earth is going to storm the beaches of Fortress Europe. And, Major, with that one we're going for broke. If they beat us back into the sea . . . " Blackford shook his head. "It may be years. Or it may be never."

"So the information we leaked must get through."

"That's right."

"Why not let it just happen?"

"What if they decide for some reason to scrub the mission?"

"That should be the mission commander's choice, sir, barring orders to the contrary."

"Normally, yes."

"And what if they got lucky? Put a bullet in old Schicklgruber?"

"I've been waiting for that one," said Blackford, smiling thinly. "Everyone assumes that Hitler's death automatically means a white flag in the West, so they can turn it all against the Russians in the East."

"It's a logical assumption, sir."

"Is it?" asked Blackford. "Assassinations have a nasty way of making heroes and martyrs out of assholes. They just might rally around the swastika and fight that much harder. And with better military leadership."

"I hadn't thought of it that way," Willis said slowly.

Blackford nodded. Point made.

"Still, those are human beings out there . . . "

Blackford turned grim. "Just what the hell do you think is going to be hitting the beaches on D-Day? By the thousands?"

Willis nodded, understanding, but . . .

"It's an old cliche," said Blackford, "but for what it's worth, command is a lonely thing. All important decisions hurt someone. But they must be made."

For a moment neither spoke.

"See if you can run down that English captain for me." said Blackford. "What's-his-name. Travis."

Hannah thought it might be Willi when she first looked out. He seemed to show up at odd times. And with the people that were there . . .

But it wasn't Willi. And whoever it was caught the movement of the curtain.

"I'm sorry to trouble you," he said when she opened the door. "I'm Heini Kruger. And I wished to inquire about the injured person."

Hannah gave him what she hoped was a dumb look. "Injured person? There's no injured . . ."

"From the cart, I mean."

But how could he know? "I'm sorry. You must be mistaken."

He looked down at the rather large stain on the step.

And Hannah felt the flush spread across her face.

"With your permission," he said, "we'll just look around." And with his hand gently but firmly in the small of her back he walked her through the house. Because that was what the Hauptsturmführer would expect him to do, under the circumstances.

Nothing.

"There?" He pointed.

Hannah laughted slightly. A nervous laugh. She knew. "Cows."

"We'll just look."

Holt was just starting back up to the loft. He'd been down stretching his legs. His mind thousands of miles away.

He'd heard the motorcycle. It'd gone on past. But then prudence . . .

"Well hello," said Kruger. Typical. Send two men to see about the same thing. And tell neither about the other. "Anything to report?"

Holt was caught flat-footed, and with his pants down. Nothing but a buckled, holstered sidearm. And he didn't speak word one of German. He smiled, made a gesture with his hand, and started on up the steps.

Kruger's senses immediately told him something was very, very wrong. A deserter, perhaps? "Stop," he said, unslinging his Schmeisser.

But Holt didn't stop.

Kruger brought his weapon to bear.

There was a click, and a spitting sound.

The submachine gun chewed up a piece of the barn near Holt.

And Heini Kruger went down quick.

154

Patch's round had caught him full in the face.

An eerie silence followed. The air was heavy with the acrid odor of gunsmoke.

"Others?" asked Patch, his P-38 still at the ready.

There was a barely perceptible tic beneath Hannah's right eye. She seemed otherwise in control. She shook her head.

The woodcutter cursed Patch under his breath, either forgetting that Patch spoke German, or not caring.

Patch paid him no heed. "Who?" he asked. "Not . . ."

"*Nein,*" said Hannah. "He asked after Herr Brüner. He'd found blood and followed . . ."

Patch pointed to Holt. "The motorcycle. Bring it in."

Holt was off.

"They'll come looking for him," said Wolff.

Patch nodded. "I know."

"Just a matter of hours," said Wolff. One combat commander enjoying the dilemma of another.

Again Patch nodded. No target in sight. The noose was tightening. He made his decision. "We're going home," he said. "We move out within the hour."

Elation. Letdown. The feeling of both at the same time.

"Hastings?"

"Yes, sir."

"Bind and gag Fräulein Müller. And hit her enough to draw blood and leave bruises."

"Sir?"

"We can't cover our sign that well. They'll know we've been here. It's her only chance. Her and her friend."

"Yes, sir."

"Joubert?"

"Oui."

"The old man'll come with us," said Patch.

Their eyes met.

"I don't know," said Patch. "Probably. For now, get rid of that wireless."

Joubert nodded.

Patch turned to Mullins, and then to Wolff. "Do what you can to make him ready to travel."

"It will kill him," said Wolff, simply.

"Probably," said Patch. "But then I have to assume he'd rather die with his own, than be shot for a spy."

Wolff nodded, understanding. "And me. Do you expect me to come this far, and then go back?"

"It's that or a bullet," said Patch. "It might've been different if we'd blown the man away, and I could see a clear run for it . . . "

"It's snowing, Major." Holt'd come back into the barn. The white stuff was glistening from his clothing.

"Much?" asked Patch.

"It'll cover the tracks."

Patch took a deep breath and let it out slowly. "Then we'll wait a few hours." It was pushing their luck. But they'd come a long way to quit five minutes before midnight. As a certain man was fond of saying.

24

"I'm not in the habit of explaining myself to company-grade officers," said Blackford. He was moving down the hall at a brisk pace. And both Major Willis and Captain Alistair Travis were at a near trot to keep up with him.

"That may be so, sir," said Travis. "but . . . "

Blackford stopped. "Then I'd suggest you check me out, Captain." And he was off again.

"I already have, sir," said Travis.

"Then you know I work for Generals Patton and Eisenhower, don't you?"

"Yes, sir."

At the door Travis showed the guard his identification, and they entered the room.

It seemed a small room. Probably because it was absolutely jammed with complicated appearing radio equipment. And though the hour was late the lights were bright, and the young British Wrens were at their work.

An older woman, a starched matronly type, came over to them. "What's this, Captain Travis?" she asked, a bit sharply.

"It's all right," said Travis. "They're cleared. Who has Johnny Cook?"

The woman looked at the logsheet she was carrying. "Yes. Eleanor has that one."

She took them over to a bright-faced young woman. They waited.

The young woman worked the key with a dexterity that was fascinating to watch. Then, finished for the moment, she removed the headset from one ear and looked at them.

"Johnny Cook," said the older woman.

"How soon do you raise them?" asked Blackford.

The young woman looked at her wristwatch, and then at the clock on the wall. "In just . . . "

"When you get them, tell them it's imperative they stay on the air until advised otherwise. Status and acknowledge. Sign it 'Blackford.' "

The young woman scribbled the message down, but even as she did so, she turned back to Blackford. Wide-eyed. "Stay on the air, sir?"

"Does everyone in the British military question the orders of a superior officer?" asked Blackford.

Neither Travis nor the older woman answered.

"Yes, sir," said the young woman.

Abruptly, Blackford turned and left the room. Willis and Travis followed.

The young woman adjusted her headset back in place, glancing at the older woman. "It's a bloody death warrant," she said.

Meyer knocked once.

"Come."

He entered, marched to the desk, clicked his heels, and waited.

"Yes?" Spaatz continued to study the papers on his desk.

"All present or accounted for, sir, save one."

At that Spaatz looked up.

"Kruger. You'll recall I sent him . . .

"Then put him on report."

"He may have been detained, sir." Meyer looked toward the window.

Spaatz followed his look. It was snowing fairly hard now. "Or someone may have detained him. Or he may have detained himself."

"Shall I give him an hour or two, and then look into it?"

Spaatz nodded. "The guests? Everything goes smoothly?"

"Very smoothly, sir," said Meyer. "Is there any chance the Führer might cancel his trip to Klessheim Castle tomorrow?"

Spaatz considered for a moment. "No, I shouldn't think so. He expects the Wehrmacht to be mobile under any conditions. And he expects no less of himself. We'll get him there. Safely. And at the hour he chooses. I assume the vehicles are ready?"

"Yes, sir. Chains on the cars. Two all-terrain trucks standing by. Everything inspected by the motorpool officer."

"And the bodyguard detachment?"

"They'll stand for your inspection at six."

Spaatz nodded. "He probably won't wish to leave before mid-morning. Perhaps later. But if he should, we'll be ready."

Hannah eased the door open. It squeaked. The candle in her hand flickered, spreading its yellow light across the barn.

Then the American major was beside her. He studied her for a moment, and then put the knife that was in his hand away.

He smiled. To reassure her. But he was tired. Drained was the word. "Something . . . ?" he asked.

"Willi was just here."

"At this time of night?"

She felt the blush. "He was just here for a short time. And he wanted to be sure and get back. With the storm."

He nodded, understanding, his eyes avoiding hers. His way of not wanting to embarrass her. And she liked him for it.

"Please go on," he said.

They were joined by the American captain. The Jew.

She took her time, to be certain she got it right. "The Führer has summoned nearly all of the high military leaders from the West. Rommel, von Salmuth . . . "

Weinberg let out a low whistle.

"And tomorrow . . . today, he will go to Klessheim Castle to have a war conference with them."

Dear God in heaven. It was really happening.

"What time?" asked Weinberg.

Hannah shook her head. "I couldn't ask many questions. But it's known that he's a late-sleeper."

Patch took out a map.

She traced the route from the Berghof to Klessheim Castle.

Patch studied the map. "Almost anywhere," he said, more to himself than to the others. "In this weather."

She watched him. The tiredness was gone. The call of battle. And she was reminded of her father. The way it must've been with him, too. The soldier. Always the soldier.

Hannah turned the wireless set on. Perhaps this would be the last time.

They'd been gone for several hours now. She'd given

them hot coffee, and bread and jam. Then they'd moved out into the blizzard. And with their white clothing they'd quickly disappeared.

A thought suddenly struck her. Even now the war might be over. No, not over. But the beginning of the end. And the end of a nightmare.

She could feel Herr Brüner's dark eyes watching her. She was sorry he'd gotten into it. But they'd said they would take him with them. Such a long ways. But that way he would be a survivor too. And maybe afterwards, he would understand.

A message was coming through now.

She put the Luger on top of the set. An old habit. She took the message down, and decoded.

Stay on the air? That was certainly strange. The man who'd taught her how to use the machine had made a rather big thing about being on the air "oh so briefly."

Status. By their way of thinking nothing had really happened yet. At least as far as she knew. So there was nothing to report. She sent that message.

Blackford. She sounded the word aloud. It meant nothing to her.

The American stirred, the Walther still in his hand. They'd given it to him just before they left. In case they didn't return.

Seconds turned into minutes.

Then they asked her to repeat. And she did.

"For Christ's sakes, lady, turn that thing off."

"Bitte?" Hannah looked at the American, wondering what it was he'd said. He was probably wanting some more water, with his fever and all. She'd get him some in a moment. Poor man.

The vehicle crept along the road in low gear.

At least as far as the driver could tell they were still on the road. They'd been stuck a good half-dozen times now. Despite the chains.

He glanced back at his two comrades.

The one with the headset smiled, and gave him the infantry sign to move forward.

The antennae on the roof of the vehicle adjusted a degree or so.

25

Take the high ground, and hold it. The maxim of the infantry, for a lot of years.

Patch looked around. It was a good spot. They looked directly down on the bend in the road. There was plenty of cover. And with a quick climb to their rear they'd again be deep in the Bavarian woods.

Even in good weather a vehicle would have to slow to make the curve. And in this weather it'd have to come to a near stop. A straight-away shot both coming and going. To miss, you'd almost have to be trying.

There'd probably be a lead vehicle. And they'd let that one go.

It really wasn't hard to kill a man, when you put your mind to it. You simply place a few charges, and blow him up.

Patch looked over at Weinberg.

Weinberg was hovering over the detonator. He was pale. Scared. But then hell, they were all scared.

And if anything was left they'd hit them again with bazookas and Schmeissers. Then in their winter white and the driving blizzard they'd just disappear.

They'd probably have radios. And they might even get out a call for help. But there wouldn't be any time. And there'd probably be a pretty fair fighting force in the vehicles themselves for that matter. But that wouldn't make any difference either.

Hit them hard. Hit them fast. And then run like hell.

Patch smiled to himself, wondering whose maxim that was. His, probably.

His stomach felt like it was in his throat. But then it was always like that before a firefight. And at such times he wondered why in the hell he did it. But then he knew why. Because when he wasn't doing it he was wishing that he was. For him, life was truly out on the edge.

The motorcade eased to a halt, supercharged engines rumbling, windshield wipers working against the snow. The flags on the fenders rippled in the now brisk wind. Drivers hopped out and began opening doors.

Hauptsturmführer Spaatz moved off to one side, to observe. It was like a piece of precision machinery. As always.

He wouldn't make the trip. He seldom did. But, rather like Bormann, he was always either present, or available.

His people came to attention. Very stiff. And very smart. No command had been given. It wasn't necessary. They were well trained.

The Führer, followed by a small entourage, came out of the Berghof.

Spaatz threw his arm in salute. And for a moment their eyes met.

Then Hitler nodded, just slightly.

His way of acknowledging a task well done. And, for Spaatz, reward enough for untiring effort.

The Führer stopped. A movie camera whirred. He seemed rather somber. Then he smiled and said something.

There was laughter.

Hitler moved on, and climbed nimbly into the front passenger seat of his red Mercedes-Benz.

The others, with Spaatz's people mingling, got into their assigned vehicles.

Doors closed, almost in unison.

The Führer smiled and waved to the cameraman.

Then the motorcade was off. For the war conference at Klessheim Castle.

Again came the command to stay on the air.

And again the American said something.

But something about it all frightened Hannah now. She turned the machine off. She picked up the Luger and stood. She was about to put the canvas back on the set and cover it with straw when she caught the movement out of the corner of her eye.

Three German soldiers had come into the barn, quietly, their weapons at the ready. They could easily have seen her, had they looked up. But they hadn't. Yet.

She disengaged the safety on the artillery Luger and sighted down the long barrel. She tried to squeeze the trigger. But she couldn't. She just couldn't. Not again.

Then the woodcutter shouted a warning.

There was a popping noise.

And a burning sensation tore through her. Her left breast. She didn't remember going down, but she found herself on her back, looking up. She could taste the blood in her mouth. And she could feel the spasms. But they seemed far away.

Then she was outside her body, leaving. She returned. Then she was leaving again.

So that was what it was like.

Then he was bending over her.

She tried to smile. "Goodbye, *mein Willi*," she said.

165

So very far away now. "I love you so.'

And this time she didn't return.

There were tears in the young German soldier's eyes. "I'm sorry," he said. And he wondered who Willi was.

Mullins watched the three German soldiers. He must look pretty bad. They'd taken one look at him and pretty much counted him out of it.

The old man's eyes never left him though. He knew about the Walther that was tucked beneath the blanket. But he hadn't said anything. He knew he'd be the first if he did.

The thing that kept going through Mullins's mind was that it hadn't been worth it. He'd left a good woman and a warm bed. And all he'd managed to do was jump out of an airplane and bust his leg. Hell, a man could do that on any given Sunday back home.

Now he was going to die in this Godforsaken, miserable place. And no one would even know where he was buried.

But maybe there was a chance. He'd have to get all three. And quick. And he'd never shot a pistol in his life. Hell, he'd barely qualified with an M-1.

Now. It was now or never.

He propped himself up, and whipped out the Walther P-38, to the utter astonishment of the three German soldiers. He squeezed the trigger. But nothing happened. The fucking safety was still on.

His strength gone, he fell back, laughing.

And they shot him.

26

"Son of a bitch," said Patch.

A vehicle was coming now. Moving fast. Too fast for the road.

A small, ugly affair — the German's idea of a jeep. The top was down. A soldier was standing up on the passenger side. Undoubtedly holding on for dear life. He'd have to be.

In the back seat a heavy machine gun swung loosely on its mount. Ready for a 360-degree field of fire.

Patch raised his hand and pointed. He shook his head.

They understood.

They would let this one go. It was just running interference. Probing. To draw fire, or whatever.

The vehicle slithered through the corner, the driver almost losing it at one point. The soldier that was standing seemed unruffled. Probably beneath his dignity to do otherwise.

"Son of a bitch," said Patch. The real thing was coming now. And his asshole felt so tight he just knew he'd never shit again. "God, I love it."

Four long Mercedes-Benz. And even at the distance you could tell there was a lot under the hood. They were moving fairly slow, and they were somewhat bunched up, considering. But that was all the better.

Three were a dark blue in color. The second Mercedes-Benz was red.

Patch took a look through his field glasses. And he could see the bastard. The silly mustache. The slop of hair over the forehead. The man responsible for the misery of millions.

Just keep coming. Just keep coming. I'm going to cut your fucking heart out.

Patch glanced at the others. They were into it in the same way.

A rifle cracked.

Oh, Jesus Christ, no. God dammit. The first car's barely . . .

Patch turned.

Weinberg was clutching his throat with both hands. And blood was squirting out between his fingers. He slumped across the detonator.

And all holy hell broke loose.

The road erupted into a cloud of dirt and snow. There was a strange hollowness to the explosions. Kind of like a firecracker going off in a trash barrel. Only more like four 90-millimeter cannons.

The lead Mercedes-Benz was literally blown apart at the seams. Bodies were tossed into the air like so many rag dolls. And parts of bodies, too. Arms. Legs.

What the hell?

Ski troops were above them, and behind them. And then they were racing down among them.

Patch grabbed his bazooka, took a quick sight-picture, and let one fly. Something struck him from behind as he did so. The last thing he saw was his rocket taking out a tree just beyond Hitler's Mercedes. A medium-sized limb slammed down across the red hood.

No one would ever say Sergeant Andrew Holt didn't do his best to kill Adolf Hitler. For the better part of an agonizing minute he stood in a half crouch emptying his Schmeisser again and again into the red Mercedes-Benz.

But Hitler's car was bulletproof. At least as far as the likes of 9-mm fodder was concerned. And though the chattering submachine gun caused the occupants of the car to huddle in fear for their lives, they were safe from harm's way that day.

The crack German ski troops everywhere now, Holt thrust the empty Schmeisser aside and took out his Walther P-38. He fought. Oh how he fought. He wanted to go home again. But even as he fought he knew such was not to be.

He'd seen Weinberg go down. And Patch. He wasn't sure about the others. And he knew he'd been hit, too.

The magazines for the Walther exhausted, he drew a fighting knife.

A German soldier was on him now. Rifle and fixed bayonet.

They circled.

Thrust and parry. Parry and thrust.

The German solider had been taught well. He feinted. Not just with the rifle and bayonet. But with his body and his eyes, too.

Holt went with it. And even as he did so he knew he'd made the fatal mistake.

The bayonet went into his breastbone to the hilt. God, it hurt so bad.

For a long moment he and the German just looked at each other.

Then, with everything he had left Holt lunged, and literally slit the German's throat from ear to ear.

Dying quickly now he fell across the already dead German. "We'll go to hell together," he said.

Sergeant Andrew Holt. And Rottenführer Willi Roehrs.

In that strange way of things, Hastings, Joubert, and Wolff were captured without firing a shot. They were suddenly surrounded, and totally overwhelmed. To come so far . . . And nothing.

To SS Colonel Max Wolff, his worst fears had now been realized. A German officer captured while aiding and abetting the enemy.

At the last minute Major Patch had given him a loaded magazine for his P-38. And he'd seriously considered trying to make a fight of it, no matter. He would have been immediately killed, of course. And the instincts for survival are strong. He'd hesitated. And now any opportunity was gone.

They'd all be executed, of course. To be found in a German uniform was enough for that.

But if . . . when they found him out, he'd be tortured. And then tortured to death.

He'd heard things. About certain people. And what had happened. And he believed them.

His eyes would be gouged out with a screwdriver. His genitalia removed with the snip of a garden shears. And then he'd be hung with piano wire. To linger.

Wolff straightened himself. Forcing himself to be calm. As he had so many times in the heat of battle.

No matter what, he must convince them that he was an Englishman, or an American. So that he would be allowed the dignity of dying like a man. Like the solider that he was.

It was late when Adolf Hitler arrived at Klessheim

Castle. Nearly 3:00 P.M. Outside, the blizzard was still raging.

General von Salmuth, commander of the Fifteenth Army on the Channel coast, was appalled by Hitler's appearance. It was an old, bent man with a pallid, unhealthy complexion who came into the room. He looked weary, exhausted — downright ill.

But though there were questions, none were asked.

Hitler still seemed to have his wits about him, however, and he soon began a one-hour speech that was delivered, several of the generals felt, with marvelous clarity and sovereign composure.

"Obviously," Hitler declared, "an Anglo-American invasion in the west is going to come. Just how and where nobody knows, and it isn't possible to speculate. You can't take shipping concentrations at face value for some kind of clue that their choice has fallen on any particular sector of our long western front from Norway down to the Bay of Biscay. Such concentrations can always be moved or transferred at any time, under cover of bad visibility, and they will obviously be used to dupe us."

Hitler warmed to his theme. "The enemy's entire invasion operation must not, under any circumstances, be allowed to survive longer than hours, or at most days, taking Dieppe as an ideal example. Once defeated, the enemy will never again try to invade. Quite apart from their heavy losses, they would need months to organize a fresh attempt. And an invasion failure would also deliver a crushing blow to British and American morale. For one thing, it would prevent Roosevelt from being reelected in the United States — with any luck, he'd finish up in jail somewhere! For another, war weariness would grip Britain even faster and Churchill, already a sick old man with his influence waning, wouldn't be able to carry

171

through a new invasion operation."

After that, Hitler showed why defeating the invasion would lead to a total Nazi victory. "The forty-five divisions that we now hold in Europe are vital to the eastern front, and we shall then transfer them there to revolutionize the situation there as soon as we have forced the decision in the west. So the whole outcome of the war depends on each man fighting in the west, and that means the fate of the Reich as well!"

27

Patch opened his eyes. His head pounded. Not since New Year's day of 1939 . . . Wolff came into focus.

"You are all right," said Wolff. He ran a finger across Patch's temple. Patch winced. "The bullet just touched you."

He helped Patch to his feet. And it was then that Patch discovered that his hands were manacled in front of him. It was the same with the other three. Something that would prove to be a mistake.

"Holt?" he asked.

Hastings shook his head.

Patch looked around. They were in a cell, in a windowless basement that had once been whitewashed. A single overhead bulb cast a yellowish light, and left dark corners. On the far wall there was a faucet with a garden hose attached. It dripped. There was a smell of feces, and of urine.

"Pray," said Patch to Joubert.

For a moment the Frenchman just looked at him. Then he understood. Sometimes the walls have ears. "Our holy Father . . ."

They talked, quietly.

Spaatz descended the stairs. Two soldiers with slung Mausers followed. Invariably he counted. He wasn't sure why. Thirteen.

It was easy to see how things might've been done differently. Now. But that was total hindsight. Nevertheless it was his responsibility. And that was the way it should be.

It might've been much worse. But it had happened.

Well, he'd been to Russia before. He didn't mind the fighting. Indeed, he was rather looking forward to that. It was the cold that he hated. But spring would come. Even in Russia winter leaves for a little while.

He would get this over with quickly.

He looked at the men in the cage. They had failed. But they had done well. He bowed slightly and clicked his heels. A gesture of respect.

"Gentlemen," he said. His English was broken. But quite understandable. "You will tell me everything about your mission."

His eyes went over them slowly. Picking out little things. Getting to know them. He would select the weakest. And he would hurt him in front of the others. Then he would take him away. The others would wonder. Their fear would build. After a while he would return and take away the leader and one other. Leaving the last one alone. And he would hurt the leader in front of the other.

And they would probably tell him everything about their mission.

He pointed to the fat one. The Frenchman. A soldier jumped to open the cell.

Joubert emerged. Standing a little straighter. Walking a little taller.

"You will cooperate," said Spaatz. "Yes?"

Joubert spit in his face. And there was a hushed awe.

174

He should not have done that.

It was Spaatz's move. He took out a handkerchief, dabbed the sputum from his face, and dropped it on the floor. Then he took out the gleaming Death's Head Luger. And he shot Joubert in the kneecap.

The explosion was deafening.

Joubert went down. The bravado was gone. He sobbed and clutched at his shattered knee.

All knew what such a wound meant.

Without a word Spaatz turned and went up the stairs.

The two soldiers followed, half carrying, half dragging Joubert.

"Bloody fucking bastard," said Hastings.

A period of time passed. Perhaps a quarter of an hour. No one knew for sure. It was waiting at its worst.

A gunshot. Upstairs.

The Hauptsturmführer working on their minds? Well, he was certainly doing that all right. But then he wasn't the kind that was given to bluffing either.

Another gunshot.

They looked at each other. And wondered about Joubert.

The door to the basement opened. The two soldiers came down.

For Patch. And for Wolff.

Try as one may, there are some things one cannot be prepared for. And what Patch and Wolff saw on being escorted into Hauptsturmführer Spaatz's office was one of those things.

Joubert was sitting in a chair near the Hauptsturmführer's desk. Both lower legs were at grotesque angles. He had been shot in the other knee. And his eyes seemed to look through them. Beyond them. But there was no luster. He had also been shot in the head.

Without seeking permission Wolff went over and closed the Frenchman's eyes. For the final sleep.

"He refused to tell me the contents of the map you saw in General Blackford's office," said Spaatz. "He was executed as a spy." He looked at his notes. "Though I believe he told me everything else, Major Patch. United States Army. Infantry."

Patch didn't answer. The map.

"And you're . . . "

Wolff met Spaatz's eyes straight on.

". . . Captain Alistair Travis."

"That is correct," said Wolff. The Frenchman had given him some breathing room.

"You don't sound English," said Spaatz. "Nor American."

"Saskatchewan, Canada."

Spaatz considered that for a moment, and then accepted it. He tapped the plastic covered map that made up the top of his desk. "Tell me about the map, Major Patch."

So it was his turn at bat. "I don't think I remember," said Patch. "The truth." They say the closer you stay to the truth, the easier it is to lie. And that was damned close to the truth. He'd been tired. And his mind'd been on Adele, and on the upcoming mission. He'd just seen it for a fraction. And then there'd been several drinks, and some bullshit.

Spaatz made a futile gesture with one hand.

The shorter of the two soldiers stood his rifle against the wall and came over. With obvious distaste he undid Patch's trousers and took out Patch's penis. Then he unscrewed the bulb from the desk lamp.

It was obvious what he was going to do. "Now just a

176

minute," said Patch. He could feel himself shriveling up.

But there was no waiting. The soldier rammed the live socket against the head of Patch's penis.

There was a hushed, spitting sound.

Patch screamed. Or he thought he did.

It was as though his penis no longer existed. The unbelievable, excruciating pulsing epicentered in his testicles, and arced everywhere.

He tried to pass out. Wanted to pass out. But he couldn't.

Then the soldier removed the lamp.

The next thing Patch remembered was looking down, to see if he'd wet himself. He was sure he had. But he hadn't. And what difference? Childhood taboos die hard.

Then the chills hit him. He shook violently.

Finally it passed. Son of a bitch. Better a bullet.

"Now?" asked Spaatz quietly.

Patch didn't answer.

The soldier reached into Patch's pants. Searched. Found what he was looking for. And exposed what he could of it.

And strangely, the thought that was going through Patch's mind was one of humor. Albeit dark humor. One more jolt, he was thinking, and there wouldn't be anything left of it. But what the hell. He wouldn't be using the damn thing anymore anyway.

The lamp started for Patch's crotch. Slowly this time. But the soldier's body telegraphed the ramming motion he was about to make.

Patch steeled hinself. But his body remembered, and revolted. No. No. No. Jesus-fucking-Christ, no. A voice. Hoarse. His. "No," he said. "No more."

Spaatz raised his hand. Just slightly.

The live socket stopped. Just short.

Spaatz tapped the desk-map.

"Don't do it," said Wolff.

Patch looked at Wolff, and at the bulbless lamp that was still in the soldier's hand. He moved to the desk. He leaned on it and studied the map.

"Bloody traitor, no!" Wolff lunged for him.

Spaatz was on his feet like a shot. The barrel of the Death's Head Luger slammed across Wolff's face. A vicious cut was opened, almost parallelling the scar. Blood streamed.

Spaatz turned back to Patch. He, too, leaned on the desk. Their faces were inches apart.

"There," said Patch, pointing. "There."

28

If it was possible to sit at a desk and talk on a telephone, and yet appear to be standing at rigid attention on a parade ground, then that was what Hauptsturmführer Spaatz was doing.

He had dictated a report to Scharenführer Meyer, setting forth in meticulous detail all that Patch had told him and shown him. The report had been transcribed, proofread, and had gone out by special messenger.

Then Spaatz had put through the telephone call.

"A matter of urgency," he had told the first person he spoke to.

Then someone else had come on the line.

"No," Spaatz had said. "It is of sufficient importance that I will speak to him personally."

There was apparently some argument against this.

"No," said Spaatz.

Then the lengthy wait began.

Wolff stood where he'd been standing since Spaatz had tried to take his head off with the Death's Head Luger. The blood on his face had dried for the most part. A guard stood to one side and slightly behind him.

Patch had asked for and received permission to go over by the window, to lean against the wall. He'd made the trip rather unsteadily.

The German solider who'd done the job on him had once again slung his Mauser, and had taken up a position just behind him. A bit inattentive perhaps.

But then Patch appeared to be on the verge of going down at any moment.

"*Heil Hitler!*" There was astonishing icy depth to Spaatz's eyes.

And there could be no doubt as to who had picked up the phone on the other end. A quiet couple of comments.

"*Jawohl, mein Führer,*" said Spaatz. "I was relieved you were spared."

A question.

And though the report was not in front of him, Spaatz launched into a near verbatim narrative of it. Neither subtracting from it, nor embellishing it. Arrows. Little flags. Beach positions. Pincer movements. A thorough man indeed. When he was finished there was silence.

The man on the other end was considering what he'd just heard. Then a simple question.

"*Jawohl, mein Fuhrer,*" said Spaatz. "I am satisfied the information is reliable." A glance at Jourbert's body, and at Patch. "It was obtained under circumstances that leave little doubt."

Something was said.

"*Jawohl, mein Führer,*" said Spatz. "*Jawohl. Danke schon, mein Führer.*" He put the phone down.

For the briefest moment, no more, Wolff's and Patch's eyes met. Now, or never.

Wolff moved to the desk. Slow. His wary guard moved with him.

Spaatz looked up.

"There is something about me that you will find interesting, Hauptsturmführer," said Wolff.

Spaatz waited.

Wolff gestured to his left arm.

Spaatz hesitated. But his curiousity was whetted. He pushed Wolff's sleeve up.

"Further."

Then Spaatz saw it. He stared at the SS blood-group number that was tattooed on Wolff's arm. Confusion in an ordered world. "Schutzstaffeln?"

An unguarded moment.

Wolff grabbed Spaatz by the head. A hand on each jaw. The connecting chain of the handcuffs against the throat beneath the chin. Fingers by the ears. Searching for, then finding the nerves, the pressure points.

Spaatz stiffened his neck, and clawed at Wolff's arms. But the grasp was a death grip.

The guard took Wolff in a bear hug, trying to pull him backwards of his commanding officer. A natural reaction. But the worst possible under the circumstances. Spaatz was pulled across his desk. Giving Wolff more leverage.

Wolff vibrated Spaatz's head. First right, then left. Getting more movement each time.

Patch's guard hesitated, and then started for the near-silent melee. He'd taken but one step when Patch drove an elbow into him. Though not commonly known, it is one of the most powerful blows a man can deliver with his arms.

A whoosh of air. The guard went to his knees. A rib, perhaps two, broken. A lung punctured, and collapsing.

Patch grabbed the Mauser rifle. A quick couple of steps. He slammed the butt into the spine of the other guard.

The guard screamed. He let go of Wolff and reached for his back. Then he went down. He lay where he fell, jerking uncontrollably.

181

A cracking noise. Like when someone works their knuckles. Only louder. Wolff let go of Spaatz.

The Hauptsturmführer slid back into his chair. His head hung limply across his heart. Though his neck was broken he was still alive. Slowly suffocating.

The door from the outer office opened. Scharenführer Meyer started into the room. "Hauptsturmführer, is everything . . . " He stopped.

The butt of the Mauser took him full in the face. Literally destroying his face.

Wolff held up the Death's Head Luger, and a small ring of keys. There was a steely glint in his eyes. One combat leader to another. Death might be just around the corner. But for now the battle was going well.

In moments they'd removed the shackles. And in less than a minute they'd brought Hastings up from the basement cell and armed him with the remaining rifle.

For a time Hastings just stood and looked at his old friend, his "mate" on so many missions.

Time was precious. But nothing was said.

Finally, with a faint smile, he touched the Frenchman on the cheek. Farewell. At least for this world. He turned to the others. "We'd best be off, hadn't we?"

The large all-terrain truck that had brought them was waiting outside. Its diesel engine clattered. Windshield wipers slapped at the snow.

The driver, the sole occupant, was behind the wheel. Probably waiting to remove their bodies.

Patch, Wolff and Hastings marched out, ramrod straight, hopefully in the best traditions of the Schutzstaffel.

The driver jumped out, and brought himself to attention.

"A matter of great urgency . . . " began Wolff.

And that was about as far as the bluff went. The driver started back into the truck for his Schmeisser.

". . . we must get to London as quickly as possible." Wolff jammed the Luger into the driver's clothing and pulled the trigger. There was little sound. Besides, a gunshot in the vicinity of the SS commandant's office was apparently not totally unheard of.

They piled into the truck, propping the driver up between them. Hastings took the wheel.

At the interior gate Wolff stuck his head out of the cab. "*Schnell, schnell*," he yelled. "Two more of the Englanders have been seen by the old Lutheran Church."

The guard on the gate began to open it. But the other guard picked up the phone.

Patch glanced at Hastings.

"Tore it from the wall, sir," said Hastings.

"They'll wonder when there's no answer," said Wolff softly. "*Schnell*," he yelled again, and began cursing.

The guard on the gate took it upon himself to open it. After all, an SS colonel . . .

The outer gate was partially open when they reached it. The word had been passed.

Then all hell broke loose. The gate began swinging shut. Evidently someone in authority had decided that the rules were not meant to be broken.

"Go," said Patch.

Hastings "stuck it in grandma" and floored it.

If the gate had been completely closed, and the reinforcing bar in place . . . And if the electric charge had been turned back on . . . But then "if" is known to be the biggest word.

The huge diesel truck took the gate out.

The guards opened fire.

Patch and Wolff returned the fire. And for a moment it

was Salerno. And Stalingrad. And Dieppe.

Then it was over.

Just the roar of the all-terrain truck. And the hush of the swirling Bavarian snowstorm.

It was over.

They would strike for Munich. Into Germany, instead of out.

There would be roadblocks. And pursuers. But it would be too late.

They would abandon the truck. And make their way on foot under the cover of the storm to a "safe-house." And then a succession of "safe-houses." Churches. Basements. Attics. Barns.

Weeks would pass.

Mission over. But I regret not accomplished, sir.

Epilogue

June 6, 1944. The announcement on the BBC just after
9:00 A.M. said it all. "Under the command of General
Eisenhower, Allied naval forces supported by strong air
forces began landing Allied armies this morning on the
coast of France."

It had begun. And it was indeed "the longest day."

Beginning at 6:30 A.M., under a heavy supporting fire,
the first of five sea-borne assault divisions had stormed
the beaches of Normandy. One hundred fifty-five thou-
sand. Omaha. Utah. Gold. Juno. Sword.

And by late afternoon there were over 10,000
casualties. Some Allied battle commanders were op-
timistic. Others were not.

In the Lion's Head Pub those who weren't "over
there," or otherwise involved in what was going on "over
there," were celebrating.

The owner was buying rounds. And at such an alarm-
ing frequency it frightened even himself.

At the crowded bar Blackford touched glasses with the
young WAC corporal next to him. She was on the plump
side. But a huge pair of breasts made her interesting
nevertheless.

He sipped the gin. Probably everyone in the place was

185

happy to be where they were. Except him.

He cocked his head to see over the crowd. Be damned. They were standing by the far window. Having a drink. Talking.

He'd wondered.

He put his glass on the bar and started to make his way over to them, rubbing against the WAC's breasts as he did so. Not intentionally. The area around the bar was that crowded.

But she took it as intentional. **And smiled.**

Well. "I'll be back," he said.

She nodded.

The British sergeant-major saw him coming, and said something to the others. They turned.

"Gentlemen," he said, as he reached them.

"Captain Travis was just telling us what you did," said Patch.

Blackford looked at Travis, and at the others. He'd walked into a lion's den. He lowered his voice. "It was necessary," he said. "Even now, the German Fifteenth is still holding at Calais. Because of what you told them."

"You fool," said Wolff.

Blackford blinked.

"A brave man took it to his grave." Wolff glanced at Patch. "And another brave man was tortured terribly."

"You didn't tell them?" asked Blackford.

"We thought the map was real," said Hastings.

"I just picked a piece of France out of the air," said Patch. "Somewhere far away, and safe."

Blackford could feel it coming.

"I told them it was Normandy."

"You told them . . . Normandy?"

"Some good men died," said Patch. "And I had the

son of a bitch in my sights. You fucking bastard." He dropped his right shoulder, telegraphing what was coming.

But Blackford was no street fighter. And he didn't know how to react.

Patch put every pound into it.

Blackford found himself flying backwards. Into a table and chairs. And onto the floor. He'd heard his nose break. Blood flowed. There was a blinding sting.

For a moment there was a hush to the Lion's Head. Then the celebration continued.

Blackford picked himself up. Holding his nose. Spitting blood. "You'll hang in Leavenworth . . ."

"You've been drinking, sir," said Travis. "You slipped. The Major tried to help."

"That's the way I saw it, sir," said Hastings.

The Nazi colonel had a thin smile on his face.

"The air's bad in here," said Patch.

Outside, the fog was so thick you could almost cut it with a knife.

Travis produced a flask and passed it around. "You had him in your sights, you said."

Patch nodded. "Another five seconds . . ."

"Would you go again?" asked Travis. "All of you?" They looked at him.

"I'd be going with you. And the man has given his word no one will fuck it up this time."

"The man?" asked Patch.

"Mr. Churchill."

The door to the Lion's Head opened and closed. The buxom Meg came over and joined them. Hastings put his arm around her.

"He's giving the bloody place away," she said. "There's no need for a barmaid."

They smiled.

"Say," she said, "I've got three lovely friends . . . "

They looked at each other.

"So what are we waiting for," said Patch. "The night's young . . . and tomorrow we may die."

High Quality Reproductions

MINER'S LAMP

A superb full size reproduction of the original coal miner's lamp. Based on the famous Davy Lamp, this working replica has been hand crafted from the highest quality brass.

To receive this magnificent lamp, just fill in the coupon below and send with cheque or P/O for £19.50 inc. VAT & P&P made payable to Book Peddlar Products. If the impossible should happen and you're not completely satisfied, just return it within 7 days and your money will be refunded in full.

Please send me _____ superb reproduction coal miner's lamp(s) within the next 21 days.

Name _____

Address _____

_____

_____

Send to: Book Peddlar Products, 16 Wood Street, Swindon, Wiltshire.

Book Peddlar Products, 16 Wood Street, Swindon, Wiltshire.

High Quality Reproductions

LACEMAKER'S LAMP

This unique and quaint lamp was developed for use by 'Cottage Industry Lacemakers'.

This superb working reproduction is exact down to the last detail including the special parabolic reflector which was used to focus the lamp light onto the delicate work patterns.

To be the proud owner of this unique reproduction lamp, just fill in the coupon below and send with cheque or P/O for £19.50 inc. VAT & P&P. made payable to Book Peddlar Products and you'll receive it within 21 days. If you are not completely satisfied, just return it within 7 days and your money will be refunded in full.

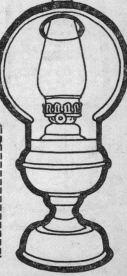

Please send me ____ unique reproduction Lacemaker's Lamp(s).

Name _____

Address_____

_____

Send to: Book Peddlar Products,
16 Wood Street, Swindon, Wiltshire.

High Quality Reproductions

HAND CANDLE LAMP

This reproduction patterned hand lamp fitted with a brass snuffer is not just a beautiful ornament.

The classic design has always been and still is a practical and mobile light source, the candle being protected from draughts by a glass cylinder capped with a brass spinning. When not in use, the snuffer is neatly attached to the side of the lamp.

This excellent candle lamp can be yours for the unbelievable price of £13.50 inc. VAT & P&P. Don't delay, fill in the coupon below enclosing cheque or P/O made payable to Book Peddlar Products and allow 21 days for delivery. If you're not completely satisfied, return it within 7 days and your money will be refunded in full.

Send me ____ Hand Candle Lamp(s)

Name _____

Address _____

_____

_____

Send to: Book Peddlar Products, 16 Wood Street, Swindon, Wiltshire.